The Adventures of
Jimmy Farrell
and the
Magic Red Ring

FRANK CAPUTO

iUniverse, Inc.
Bloomington

The Adventures of Jimmy Farrell and the Magic Red Ring

This is a work of fiction. All of the characters, names, incidents,
organizations, and dialogue in this novel are either the products
of the author's imagination or are used fictitiously.

iUniverse books may be ordered through booksellers or by contacting:

iUniverse
1663 Liberty Drive
Bloomington, IN 47403
www.iuniverse.com
1-800-Authors (1-800-288-4677)

ISBN: 978-1-4759-4182-1 (sc)
ISBN: 978-1-4759-4183-8 (hc)
ISBN: 978-1-4759-4184-5 (e)

Library of Congress Control Number: 2012913915

Printed in the United States of America

iUniverse rev. date: 8/17/2012

I would like to thank my wife Debra, Jennifer our daughter, Michael our son (may he rest in peace), and the rest of my family and friends for believing in me. They are my inspiration! They are my motivation!

Many thanks to Joseph Caputo for the cover illustration and design. And to Nicole Caputo for chapter illustration and editing.

BACK WHEN THE ADVENTURE BEGAN

"Walk faster. It's almost dark, and your father wants you home by sunset," the tall American Indian said as he passed young Mike and Ron on the trail.

Jo-Pac reached back and patted the top of Mike Farrell's head. "Golden hair is too heavy. It makes you walk slow. You must eat good food to get strong. When you are strong like me, your hair will look like this." He teased the two thirteen-year-old boys as he shook his head so that the shoulder-length jet black hair whipped around.

Mike stopped, took a deep breath, and raised a hand to sweep the blond curls from his sweaty forehead. "Slow down, Jo," he said to the Indian. "We're almost there."

Exhausted from their long day of fishing, Mike and his friend Ron Phlegmats set their fishing rods and tackle down by the brush. They folded their arms and sat down on the trail.

Jo-Pac looked back. "Okay, we will take a small rest if you boys are tired," he said as he walked back to where the boys were sitting.

Suddenly, Ron's face turned cold with fear as he pointed to the direction of a rustling noise. "What's that sound?"

"Look out!" Mike cried as a man appeared from out of the brush.

Jo-Pac turned around and was met with the butt of a rifle.

Bam! He went down to the ground. He was out cold. Seconds later he came to, scrambled to his feet and called to the boys. He was met with the tip of the same rifle pointed right between his eyes.

"One move, Injun, just one move and I'll blow your dang head clear off," the sheriff said as he kicked Jo-Pac back to the ground. About a dozen rough-shaven, pot-bellied men came out of nowhere and surrounded Jo-Pac on the trail.

"Let him go," Mike said.

"He didn't do anything wrong," Little Ron added.

The men in the posse laughed, all showing nearly toothless smiles as they took turns kicking at Jo-Pac.

"Hear that, Injun? These here youngsters think ya ain't done nothin wrong. I reckon they don't know Injuns," one of the men said as he loosened up the wad of tobacco in his mouth and spat it at Jo-Pac. "There ain't an Injun that ever done anything right. They ain't nothing but thieves and murderers, boy, thieves and murderers."

The posse dragged Jo-Pac out of the woods and into the road in front of Mike's house. Mike and Ron followed helplessly. Two of the men went behind a patch of trees to drive out the trucks that were hidden there earlier. The others taunted Jo-Pac as if playing a game of name-calling.

Tears filled Mike's eyes as he ran over to Jo-Pac and hugged him, putting himself between Jo-Pac and the abusers.

The largest of the men stepped up. "Cork" was his name. He pulled Mike away by the arm and flung him to the ground. "That's enough, boy, this here Injun's a killer. He's lucky we don't just string him up right now."

A shot rang out, and the posse turned in the direction of the gunfire. Mike's father, John Farrell, walked over from the farmhouse holding a rifle in his hand, ready to shoot again.

"What the heck is going on here?" he demanded as he pointed his rifle at the man who had thrown his son to the ground. "You want to try that on me, Cork?" he said to his grubby, soil-covered neighbor.

"You best mind your own business, Farrell; this here's official police business. That filthy Injun just killed a man in cold blood, not two hours ago," Cork said as he opened his chew packet and put a new wad in his mouth.

"That's a lie, Dad!" Mike shouted. "Jo has been with us all day. We were fishing."

"That's right, Cork," John Farrell said. "I watched them leave this morning, and if my son said he was with them all day, then he was."

"What about you, John? Were you with them, too?" the sheriff asked, as he walked up pushing the tip of John's rifle toward the ground. "Cause there's a witness says this here Injun pulled the trigger."

The sheriff snickered as he motioned his men to put Jo-Pac in the police car. "I guess we gonna let the judge decide if these here two boys is telling the truth, or that old widow who seen it happen."

John Farrell and the two boys watched as the posse dragged their friend to the car and threw him in the back seat. Jo-Pac gazed out the window at his only friends in the white world as the car drove away.

"What's going to happen now?" Mike asked.

"You might have to testify," his father answered. "Think you can handle it, son?"

"You bet, Dad. I'll show them."

"I'll show them, too," Ron said.

CHAPTER 1

MAGIC BLOOMS

That was a long time ago. Mike Farrell was a grown man now. He and his father never forgot the injustice on that day more than thirty years ago. At the time the Farrells had known Jo-Pac for only a couple of weeks, but he quickly became a part of their family. When he was released from prison ten years ago, the Farrells made sure he had a job and a place to live. He was once again a good friend to the family, especially Mike's son Jimmy, who was now a young man of thirteen.

Jimmy was always looking for something exciting to do in that small town just east of the Delaware River. The whole area was full of caves and woods, a perfect place for an adventurous young man. When he wasn't getting into mischief, he was visiting with Jo-Pac.

Jo-Pac, always a quiet man, pretty much kept to himself now. Hardly any of the townspeople associated with him. Mike Farrell, Ron

Phlegmats and their parents were the only ones who believed Jo was innocent of the crimes that sent him to prison.

Even though Mike and Ron swore that Jo-Pac was with them on that day all those years ago, the court didn't believe them because of their ages. But that was all in the past. Jo was a hard-working member of the community now. Still, the townspeople pointed and whispered. If it wasn't for Mike Farrell, Ron Phlegmats and their parents, he would have received no welcome home at all.

Jo-Pac had been a good friend of the two families since then and spent a lot of time with Mike's son, Jimmy, as he was growing up. The two of them would sit on Jo-Pac's porch, and Jimmy would listen to stories about the different Indian tribes that lived around the area.

One late spring afternoon while walking through the field, Jimmy saw a bunch of flowers blooming at the bottom of a hill near a stream behind his family home. They had a bright red blossom, with outer petals like tulips and center buds that looked like roses.

"Wow!" he said, going down for a better look. "I've never seen flowers like this before. I'll take one over to Jo's house. He'll know what they are; he knows everything about this whole countryside."

Jo-Pac was sitting in his rocker on the porch. As Jimmy approached, he swung his long gray hair back, and put his old brown suede hat on.

"Hey, Jo!" Jimmy shouted as he reached the porch and extended the flower to him. "Did you ever see anything like this before?"

"Why sure." Jo-Pac sat back in his chair and smiled. "That's the Magic Red Ring flower of the Takoda Indian tribe."

"You never told me about them."

"Well, how about if I tell you about them right now? Would you like that?"

"Sure thing," Jimmy answered.

Jo-Pac told his story:

"Well, the Takoda Indian tribe lived somewhere along our stream a long time ago. They were a peaceful tribe and would rather run from a fight than take another life. But when hostile tribes confronted them, they had to fight. If they didn't, their attackers would kill all the men, and put the women and children into slavery.

"One day, the chief called for the medicine man and told him to find a way to make his people invisible to their enemies, so they wouldn't have to fight. After many tries, the medicine man mixed a brew of many kinds of flowers and herbs. He enchanted the mixture, and then poured the magical mix on the ground. A couple of weeks later there grew a flower, and the Chief called it the 'Magic Red Ring' flower. When the tribal members ate a piece of its bulb, they didn't become invisible, but shrank to about the size of a fist. That worked out very well for the tribe, even better than being invisible.

"The Takoda Indians built a small shelter out of stone and clay. They made it strong enough to withstand almost anything and always kept it full of supplies. When trouble was near, or when big storms were coming, they ate the Red Ring Flower bulbs and shrank down to escape to their shelter. When the trouble passed, all they had to do was eat the bulb, and they would grow back to normal size."

"So, Jo, you mean that if I eat this bulb, I will shrink down to a miniature me?"

"Not necessarily, Jimmy. Only the plants that have a red ring in the bulb have the power to shrink. Anyway, that's what they say. I've never seen one with a red ring in the bulb."

"Let's look at this one," Jimmy said as he handed over the flower that he had pulled out of the ground, bulb and all.

Jo-Pac reached into his pocket and took out his knife and cut the bulb in half from side to side. He let the knife linger while he explained to Jimmy that the bulb had to be cut from side to side to see the magic.

"Come on, come on, let's look at the bulb," Jimmy blurted out.

"You see?" Jo-Pac separated the two halves. "If this were one of the flowers with the power to shrink, there would be a bright red ring right around the center of the bulb."

"Have you ever found one?" Jimmy asked.

"No, I never really looked. Well… maybe once or twice, but I don't think they exist anymore, so we shouldn't kill these beautiful flowers looking for something that has vanished."

"Do you really think there were such Indians?"

"Of course. At least that's what my father and grandfather told me."

That night, Jimmy couldn't sleep imagining how cool it would be to find one of those Magic Red Ring flowers.

The next day was the last day of school. The story was still burning in his head on the bus ride home from school. Jimmy told his friend Tommy all about the Takoda Indian tribe while they made plans for the weekend, the same plans they made every weekend they were able to. They were going to camp out in the backfield, not too far from Jimmy's house, right near the stream. It was just going to be two friends camping, hiking and fishing all weekend, and maybe a little longer if the weather held up.

It was about five o'clock in the afternoon by the time camp was set up, so they gathered some fire wood and built their fire before they went fishing for their dinner. Both boys were regular campers and knew everything they needed to know about camping safety. Tommy's father was a Scout leader, and the two boys were his best students. The boys set out in different directions to go fishing when Jimmy noticed another bunch of the Red Ring flowers. He looked down at them and smiled in disbelief as he walked past them.

Takoda Indians, he thought. But then he stopped and turned back to the flowers, and his smile became a curious look as he stared down at them. "I wonder—could it be?" He knelt down and picked one out of the ground. "After all," he said, "this bunch could be the magic ones."

He took out his pocketknife and cut the bulb the same way Jo-Pac had showed him. He was smiling as he separated the two halves of the bulb. In an instant Jimmy went from smiling to total surprise.

"Tommy! Come here! I found one," he yelled as he ran at full speed back to where Tommy was fishing. "I found one. The story is true."

"Found one what?" Tommy asked as they met in camp.

"A real Magic Red Ring flower. You know, the story I told you on the bus today. See for yourself. Look inside," he shouted as he handed the bulb to Tommy.

Tommy looked at the bulb, and took a deep breath. "I see, all right. I see that you better get your eyes checked."

"What do you mean?" Jimmy grabbed the bulb out of Tommy's hand and took another look. The red ring was gone. It looked just like the one Jo-Pac had cut in half, no ring and no magic.

"There was a red ring. It was plain as day," Jimmy cried as he tossed the two halves to the ground.

Tommy teased him for a couple of minutes. Then they went back to fishing. They caught four small trout, just enough for dinner, along with the cornbread that Jimmy's mom had baked. They sat around the fire eating dinner and talking about the Takoda Indian tribe and the Red Ring flower.

"I'm telling you, Tommy, there was a red ring in that bulb. I'm not kidding."

"Well, if there was a red ring, you must have lost it before you showed it to me. I think you believe Jo's stories a little too much. Whoever heard of a flower that makes you smaller if you eat it?"

"It's not the flower, Tommy. It's the bulb that makes you shrink, the bulb with the red ring."

"Okay, whatever. I'm tired, I'm going to sleep. Good night." Tommy said as he crawled into the tent.

"Good night, Tommy," Jimmy replied. He put out the fire, then followed behind.

They talked on and off through the night about what all the boys in their class talked about: Betty Ann Phlegmats and how they each loved her more than anything. She always wore a pretty dress to school, and her curly blonde hair was always tied in tails. Every time one of them stopped talking about her, the other started. Neither one of them got much sleep that night.

Saturday was a bright sunny day and they were both up early enough to greet the sunrise. They crawled out of the tent, stumbled to their feet, and walked over to the firewood. The boys started a fire to get rid of the early morning chill. It wasn't until the fire was lit and the cocoa was poured that the early birds got a real look at one another. They both laughed, pointing at each other's morning hair.

Tommy's rust-colored straight hair pointed in about twenty different directions away from his head. One of his eyes was squinting while the other seemed to sag just enough to make him look as if he was ready for a nap.

Jimmy had a totally different morning look. His wavy blond hair was fine on one side, and the other side looked like it had been glued tightly against his head. But his eyes were both the same—wide open, as if he were doing all he could to keep them that way.

When their hot cocoa was finished, they planned the day as they came to life. They were going to find a good spot to fish for a while, have a trout lunch along with some leftover cornbread, and then hike up the stream looking for old Indian artifacts. On a hike last year, they found a really cool arrowhead and had been searching for more ever since. They left camp with their fishing rods in one hand and their tackle boxes in the other.

"Hey, Tommy, did you take some of the trail bars in case we get hungry before the first catch?" Jimmy asked jokingly, as he was sure that they would catch fish as soon as they dropped hooks into the stream.

"Don't worry, I got them." And since they always razzed each other on who was a better fisherman, Tommy added, "You know we're not going to need them, I'm fishing. Now if you were by yourself, you would need a whole bunch, or you would starve."

"Yeah, right. Why don't we go downstream on the other side by the slate cliff? There's that nice deep pool over there. We can just cast out our lines and relax, you know, catch a couple of Z's."

Tommy smiled as he followed behind. "Sounds good to me."

About half way down the path to their fishing spot, Tommy saw a patch of those flowers. "Look, is that them? Your magic flowers?"

"All right, don't rub it in. I wish I'd never told you about the Red Ring flower."

Tommy went over to the flowers, put his tackle box down and pulled one out of the ground. "Come on, Jimmy, let's check it out. Maybe we can shrink down just a little bit. It'll really make catching fish a lot more fun. Just think of the fight we can get out of a trout when we are half size."

He laughed as he put down his rod, took his knife out, and cut the bulb in half. As he separated the bulb and looked at it. To his amazement, he saw a bright red ring around the center.

"You're right, Jimmy. I see it. I see the red ring. I can't believe it. That old Indian was right, there really are little Indians, aren't there?"

"All right, Tommy, good one, but enough is enough. I thought we were going to forget about all that. Let's just go fishing."

"I'm not kidding. Here, look for yourself," he said as he threw the two halves over to Jimmy.

Jimmy dropped his gear and caught the two halves, and then he inspected them. "Very funny, can we just go fishing now?"

"What are you talking about, Jimmy? We have proof, we found the red ring."

"The joke's over, that was a good one," Jimmy said as he tossed the bulb back at Tommy's feet. "Can we go fishing now?"

One of the halves rolled right side up in front of Tommy. The red ring was gone. Tommy picked it up shaking his head in disbelief. "It must have disappeared. It was there, I promise."

"That's it!" Jimmy shouted. "It disappeared, that's exactly what the chief wanted it to do. The medicine man must have been on the right track. The ring disappears, not the person who eats it. That's why you didn't see it when I cut it open. It disappeared by the time I got back to show you. And that's why I didn't see it when Jo cut it open, he spent all that time explaining how to cut the bulb.

"What are you blabbering about, Jimmy? What medicine man? What chief?"

"Didn't you pay any attention to what I was saying on the bus yesterday? Or did you spend all your time staring at Betty Ann and tuning everything else out?"

Tommy answered, "I was tuning everything out, everything but Betty Ann. Sorry, I only caught bits and pieces of the story."

Jimmy gave him a recap and pulled out another flower. "If I'm right, there is going to be a bright red ring around the center of this bulb. If I'm wrong, I am just as crazy as you say I am. Let's see."

He cut open another bulb and separated it in front of Tommy. They both looked down at the brightest red ring ever. They continued staring at it, speechless until it disappeared before their very eyes. They looked up at each other, shrugged their shoulders and went without speaking for a couple of minutes.

Jimmy broke the silence as he gripped the bulb in his hand. "I'm not crazy, and neither is Jo. The Takoda Indian tribe really existed. They lived somewhere along this stream, and they had one heck of a talented medicine man."

They stared at it for a little while longer, each caught up in his own fantasy about what it would be like to be only a couple of inches tall.

"What do we do now, Tommy? Do we tell somebody? Should we go get Jo?"

Tommy put his arm around Jimmy and smiled. "Let's eat one and see what happens to us. Let's see if the stories are true. Just think of the great time we could have, we can go mountain climbing on a rock that was only a couple of feet high, we can eat one candy bar for a month, we can ride on the back of a turtle. There is no end to what we could do with these things, not to mention the profit we stand to make when we market our find as a weight-loss product."

Jimmy stared at him as he continued blurting out all the possibilities of a thirteen-year-old boy being four inches tall, and all the ways they could spend the money they were going to make.

"Hold on, Tommy. We're not selling these, and we can't just take one and shrink down. What if it's poison, or what if it tastes horrible, or what if … ?"

Tommy put his hand over his friend's mouth, stopping him from saying another word. "What's the matter, Jimmy? Are you chicken?"

That was all Jimmy needed to hear. He could not stand being called a chicken. He immediately took a bite of one of the bulbs and handed the other to Tommy. "Your turn," he said as he chewed and swallowed.

Tommy looked at Jimmy for a second or two as if waiting for something to happen. "How do you feel Jimmy? Is anything happening? Do you feel anything at all? How does it taste? Is it good?"

Jimmy looked at him and smiled, and then he rubbed his stomach. "Tastes great, and I feel great. Going to join me, or not?"

Tommy took a bite, chewed and swallowed. "Gr-r-oss," he spouted and spat to get the flavor out of his mouth. "This is awful. Why did you say it was good?"

Jimmy just smiled back at him. They both stood there quietly, waiting to see some results.

Tommy was the first to come back to reality. "Great story, Jimmy, but the only thing that is shrinking is my faith in folktales. Let's go, I want to catch some fish before lunchtime or else we're going to have to eat these trail bars, or maybe even a couple of these bulbs."

They threw down what was left of their halves, picked up the gear and walked across the stream to their fishing spot. Both of the boys climbed on top of the slate cliff closest to the water and sat on the edge, feet dangling about a foot or two above the calm water. They baited the hooks and dropped their lines in the water. Soon they were talking about the Red Ring flower again, still imagining what they would do if they were that small. Within minutes, they were both asleep as the fish began to nibble the bait from their hooks.

CHAPTER 2

THE MAGIC BEGINS

It wasn't long before Tommy woke up stretching and yawning. "I feel great. I feel like I slept for two days straight. What about you? How did you sleep? Jimmy, wake up."

He turned, about to shake Jimmy to wake him up, but no one was there. "Jimmy!" he shouted. "Where are you? Where did you go?"

"Stop yelling. I'm right over here."

Tommy turned to his other side, and there was Jimmy, climbing over a log that was sitting between the two boys. "Where did that come from?"

"What?" Jimmy replied.

"That log. Where did it come from? I didn't see it when we got here."

They both looked at the log in confusion, then down the trunk.

"I don't know, Tommy. We would have heard it fall down while we were sleeping."

Tommy stood up with Jimmy, and they walked along the trunk until they came to a point where thick wire was tied around the tree.

"It must be a telephone pole, or an electric pole, it must have come down during a storm. You know, these power lines go right through the property," Jimmy said as if he were trying to convince himself.

Then they looked the other way. Jimmy rubbed his eyes. Tommy began to shake and hit the side of his head as if he were trying to wake himself up or knock some sense into himself. They slowly walked back the other way beside the trunk until they came to what seemed to be a spool of telephone wire tied to the tree.

But it wasn't telephone or electric wire, and it wasn't a telephone or an electric pole. It was a pole, all right, but it was a fishing pole. It was Jimmy's fishing pole. And it was about a mile long, or so it seemed.

"What's going on, Jimmy? I think I'm freaking out."

"You're not freaking out. Can't you see? The Magic Red Ring Flower bulbs really work. I can't believe it. Look at us. Look where we are," Jimmy roared as he looked at their surroundings with fascination at how everything looked from this new perspective.

"What are you smiling about, Jimmy? We're in a lot of trouble. What are we going to do? How are we going to get back to our regular size?"

Jimmy kept calm, as if he transformed all the time. "Easy. We just eat another one of those bulbs and pop up to size. Sometimes, Tommy, I don't know if you think before you talk."

Tommy walked over and got right in Jimmy's face. "Oh, yeah, you don't know if I think before I talk? Well, do you think before you talk? Do you, Jimmy? I don't think so. If you did you would remember that we are on one side of this once small stream, but now raging river. And, oh yeah, the plants. Excuse me, the flowers are on the other side. Now, you were saying?"

Jimmy's expression turned to match the scared feeling he was starting to get. "I was saying that we are in a world of trouble, and I totally blame you. If you hadn't called me a chicken, we never would have been way down here."

Tommy said, "Think back. It was you who started this whole thing, with your stupid Indian stories."

"All right, Tommy. We're in this together, so let's just work it out, okay? First we have to make, you know, a plan of action. Then we have to gather supplies, like food, rope, tools we might need, clothes. Hey, that's right. How is it that our clothes shrunk with us?"

Tommy patted his jeans, which were now tightly woven denim. "I don't know, maybe it's because they were touching us. That must be it. See, my boot knife shrank down with us, and the lighter for campfires in my pocket shrank, too."

Jimmy felt his pocket and pulled out his own lighter. "That's a good start. Now all we need is a few more things and we can get on our way. We're going to have to get some stuff out of the tackle box. I hope I left it open. If not, it may take us the rest of the day just to open it."

"Look over there," Tommy pointed. "The tackle box, and it's open."

The tackle box was a lot farther away than it looked. With a little grunting and groaning, they got hold of the rim and lifted themselves over the side. Once inside they rummaged through all the tackle, being careful not to get hooked, looking for what they could use for their trip back to the flower patch.

They found thin fishing line that could be used as rope and small hook bags that could be used as backpacks. The biggest find was a small treble hook; the three-hook set up used on fishing lures would be perfect if they needed to do any climbing. They climbed out of the box with their gear, jumped to the ground, and sat down to go over the plan.

"All right," Jimmy said, showing he had calmed down and was

17

thinking clearly. "First we climb down this mountain of slate, but not too close to the water. Then we make our way downstream to where that big tree fell last month."

"But that's way past the flowers." Tommy said, "It'll take us forever."

"Well, it's either that, or try swimming across. Didn't you say this stream is now a raging river? You know, we'll probably have to dodge the trout who think we look like big flies, or grubs, not to mention those big crawfish who could probably eat us both and still be hungry. So what's it going to be?"

"Well Jimmy, when you put it that way, it's really not that far. Looks like me and you are going on a little hike. But before we go, let's get something to eat. It's almost lunchtime, and I'm hungry."

"You're right, we should build up our energy. It's going to be a long trip. Where are those trail bars? Didn't you have them in your pocket?"

"Yeah, they're right here," Tommy said, reaching for the side pocket of the vest that he wasn't wearing. "Oh, no," he said with disappointment on his face. "They were in my vest pocket, and I took the vest off."

"No big deal. Where did you put your vest? Tommy, where did you put your vest?"

Tommy slowly looked up and pointed to the vest hanging on a branch that extended over the slate cliff. "There it is, and there's our lunch, only about a mile straight up."

Jimmy looked up and smiled. "It's not that bad. All we have to do is climb along the branch and down into your pocket. See, your pocket is even open and there's our lunch sticking out. Let's go. We'll be there in no time. We can eat lunch now and even pack some to take with us. I'm sure there will be some left over." They laughed, looking up at a trail bar about the size of a car.

The branch was tilted almost touching the ground, so they were able to jump on it and walk up to the vest as if they were climbing a hill. Once they were inside his pocket, Tommy pulled out his knife and began to cut through the trail bar wrapper.

"This is going to be good. They're usually stingy with the chocolate chips in these things, but today I get all the chocolate I want."

He cut a hole through the wrapper large enough for them to get their hands in. They took hold of one edge and ripped it open.

"Wow," Jimmy said, "look at that. We can eat for months and still have leftovers. Look at the oatmeal grains, just one would be enough for a whole meal."

Tommy jumped over to one side of the gigantic bar and clutched one of the chocolate chips sticking out on the side. "Have you ever seen anything so wonderful? You can have your oatmeal. I'll have the chocolate chips," he said as he dug at it with his trusty knife.

They sat and enjoyed their feast, then rested to let it all settle. Jimmy stood and packed a hook bag made into a duffel bag with some oats and a few raisins.

"Hey, Jimmy, don't forget to put some chocolate chips in our lunch bag."

Jimmy carried the bag over and put it down by Tommy's feet. "Here you go. Take as many as you want. You're going to carry the food bag. I'm going to carry the gear bag that's down by our rods."

After Tommy loaded the bag with some chocolate chips, they climbed down the mesh fabric of the vest like a ladder until they were close enough to the ground to drop off. As they were approaching the tackle box, Jimmy picked up the gear bag and flung it over his head. That's when one of the fishing rods began to shake as if something was pulling it.

"Hey, Jimmy, we got a fish. Let's see how big it looks," Tommy said while running toward the edge of the cliff.

"No! Don't! Come back!" Jimmy yelled franticly. "Don't go too close to the edge."

But Tommy kept on going until he reached the edge. "Wow, you have got to see this. It's beautiful," he said as he gazed down at the stream through the eyes of a four-inch boy. "And we didn't get a fish, all we got was a stick."

At the end of the fishing line a piece of branch was rubbing against the bare hook as it drifted downstream, just about to reach some faster moving water. Jimmy came to the edge on the other side of the rod and looked down at a disaster waiting to happen.

He yelled over to Tommy in a state of panic. "Watch out! Get out of the way!"

It was too late. The branch hit rough water just as the hook caught on. The force of the fast-moving water was enough to drag the fishing rod toward Tommy. It slammed right into him, knocking him off the cliff and into the pool below. Tommy and his lunch bag fell into the water, and then there was silence.

Jimmy just stared down at the ripples of water below waiting for Tommy to emerge. There was nothing. Tommy wasn't coming up.

"Oh no," Jimmy cried out as he dove off the cliff and into the water after his friend.

A few seconds later, Jimmy came up holding onto Tommy with one arm and swimming with the other. He knew there wasn't much time before they hit that fast current, so he had to swim hard. Holding onto his unconscious friend, he made it over to a floating branch and pushed Tommy up on it. As he tried to pull himself up, the whole branch was jerked forward out of his reach and into the current. The branch and Tommy were headed downstream fast.

Within seconds, he lost sight of Tommy and was being thrown around by the fast current. He lost all sense of direction, he didn't even know which way was up. For each second he was above water, he seemed to spend two below. The water wasn't getting any calmer. He was being slammed into rocks, sticks and whatever else happened to be in the stream. He was about to give up when the water slowed down enough for him to make his way to the side. Exhausted, battered and confused, he pulled himself ashore and just collapsed on the side of the stream.

He woke up surprised at how slowly he was moving. How could a trip downstream take so much out of him? He felt like he had just played twenty-seven innings of baseball against a really good team. He sat up rubbing his eyes, still a little dazed, and then he looked around panic-stricken.

"Oh, no! Where's Tommy?"

He jumped to his feet and ran to the edge of the water, climbing on top of a stone for a better view. He had to find Tommy and had to make sure he was okay. He jumped off the stone and ran downstream looking around, totally lost in his surroundings, and at the same time getting used to seeing everything from a small point of view. He kept searching for anything that would let him know his friend was all right.

Up ahead he saw something small. Not sure what it was, he ran over to inspect. "Oh no," he gasped as he bent over to pick up the ripped bag of crumbs that Tommy was carrying when he fell in the water. Oats and chocolate chips had spilled out and were everywhere. He didn't know it then, but that meant trouble for him. He held the empty pack in his hand, looking over the surrounding area for some sort of clue as to what had happened to Tommy.

All of a sudden, BAM! He was hit from behind with a force that he had never felt before. It picked him up off the ground and threw him into the air. He landed, rolled a couple of times and crashed into a moss covered rock that cushioned the blow. He stood up off-balanced and turned around to see the biggest crawfish ever. The monster was walking toward him, eating the spilled contents of the backpack as it came closer and closer.

He tried to overcome his fright by making light of the situation. "I never used you guys for bait. I just wanted you to know that before you run out of food over there."

He looked around for a quick exit, but it was hopeless. He was surrounded on three sides by rocks too high for him to scale. The only way out was past the giant sweet-freak who was eating all the chocolate chips and leaving the healthy oats behind.

"Take it easy on that stuff, you don't want to get all strung out on sugar," he whispered, trying to forget that he might be the dessert.

Finally, the thing looked at Jimmy as it put the last piece of chocolate in its mouth. It started walking toward him. Jimmy backed up trying to blend into the wall of rocks, pointlessly looking on the ground for something to defend himself with. The crawfish stood up on its back legs and extended its claws. The monster opened a claw and snapped it a few times, a sign that it was still hungry.

Just as it started to swing its open claw down at Jimmy, a stick came flying from above the wall of rocks behind him. The stick flew right into the monster's neck, then another. The third one hit the monster in the head, bringing him down to his death. Jimmy then realized that the sticks were arrows.

It must be Tommy. "Hey, Tommy," he called up over the rocks. "Nice shot. Where did you get the stuff to make a bow and arrow? We are going to have one heck of a crawfish dinner tonight." He ran around to the other side of the rock wall to greet Tommy but was shocked, amazed, at what he saw.

Standing before him, dressed in a loincloth and moccasins, complete with bow and arrow and a feather tied to his head, was an Indian. A tall, dark, stone-faced Indian, the same size as Jimmy and standing face-to-face with him.

"An honest-to-goodness Indian, right here in my own backyard? Well, this really isn't my backyard anymore. This is a hostile, wooded region somewhere in the miniature world that is my backyard. And you're a, an Indian. Wait a minute, you're one of those Takoda Indians with the Magic Red Ring. It's true. I knew Jo was telling the truth even if he didn't know himself."

All of Jimmy's fear was replaced by a thousand questions. He couldn't wait to start asking all the questions, but nothing would come out.

"Sure," he thought, "Jo said they were a friendly tribe, against violence and all that. But what if I got the oddball?"

He couldn't think with all the worry, so he said the first thing that came to his mind. "I come in peace."

Immediately, he slapped himself on the side of the head. "Now I sound like a science fiction movie."

The Indian started walking toward Jimmy, as he drew a big knife from a sheath tied around his waist.

CHAPTER 3

THE SLATE MOUNTAIN

"How do you know of Magic Red Ring? Tell me," the Indian said as he walked past Jimmy to the crawfish and cut his arrows out of the hard shell. He put the arrows into a leather pouch tied to his back, returned his knife into the sheath on his waist, and walked back over to Jimmy.

"How do you know Magic Red Ring?" he repeated as he looked Jimmy over.

"Look, I'm a friend, I don't want any trouble. My friend Jo told me about the Red Ring flower, and the myth about the Takoda Indian tribe. Well, I guess it's really not a myth anymore. I'm standing right in front of you, so you must be real. Anyway, when me and my friend Tommy... Tommy! You have to help me, my friend, he's hurt and floating down the stream on a branch." Jimmy began to run around, looking in all directions for a clue about where Tommy was.

The Indian stopped Jimmy. He put his hand on Jimmy's back, guiding him in the direction of a path along the stream. "Come, I will help you find friend."

They walked up the path a bit, and there, tied to a branch, was a dark brown horse.

"I don't believe my eyes. Is that what I think it is? Is that a miniature horse?"

The Indian stopped and looked over at Jimmy. "What means this word, miniature horse?"

Jimmy thought about it for a second or two and said, "Well, it kind of means very, very, very small."

The Indian nodded his head. "Yes, it is miniature horse. And miniature boy and miniature brave." He looked back in the direction they came from. "Not miniature so-ga," he said, pointing to the crawfish.

They both laughed as the Indian untied the horse and led the way downstream.

"So what's your name, sir?"

The Indian put his hand on his chest and proudly introduced himself. "I am called Yuma, Chief Yuma, son of Chief Jolon, son of Chief Paco before him. What are you called?"

Jimmy frowned at hearing a whole line of these authentic Indian names. It seemed his name was missing something.

"I'm just Jimmy, plain old Jimmy."

"Plain Old Jimmy is good name."

Just as Jimmy was about to explain that "plain old" was not part of his name, Yuma stopped him.

"Friend was there." He led the way to a small piece of light blue chambray cloth stuck on a branch by the side of the stream. Jimmy pulled the cloth off the branch and held it out to inspect it.

"It's a piece of his shirt. This is the branch he was on when I lost him in the rough water. What am I going to do? I can't go home without him."

"Plain Old Jimmy, I think I know where friend is. Come with me."

Yuma rushed over to the horse and jumped on. "Give me hand," he said as he extended his hand down.

Jimmy grabbed on, and in one swift movement Yuma pulled him onto the horse and took off into the woods. They were moving so fast that Jimmy was scared to watch and closed his eyes. When they slowed down, Jimmy opened them and saw the horse was still headed downstream.

None of the surrounding area was familiar to him. He thought, *From down here, I wouldn't know if we were in my mother's garden. Yes, I would. Everything would be dead.* He laughed out loud at his mother's lack of a green thumb.

He wondered if they had traveled off of the family's property into Horace Phlegmats' domain, as he called the Phlegmats' family farm. Horace Phlegmats was the craziest, meanest, most horrible man in the town. He was also Betty Ann's uncle. He worked the farm for Betty Ann's father, Ron Phlegmats, but they were two totally different people. Betty Ann's father was the nicest guy in town. For the longest time, he and Jimmy' s father were the only ones who called Jo-Pac their friend. Nobody knew how Ron Phlegmats' brother Horace turned out so different. It was said that if he saw you on the property, he would sic the dogs on you. He had two of the meanest Rottweilers ever, Satan and Lucifer, who everyone called the "Demon Dogs."

Now Jimmy didn't know where he was, and the Demon Dogs were on his mind. "Where are we going, Yuma? I don't know if this is a good idea."

"It is all right, Plain Old Jimmy, we are almost there."

They followed a trail along the stream and turned off into the woods. Suddenly right in front of them was a huge mountain of layer-upon-layer of slate.

They got off the horse at the foot of the mountain, and Yuma led it by the reins over a worn path that seemed to have been well traveled. The path led to a crevasse where three or four layers of slate met, and one layer hung over their head. Another layer had a crack wide enough to drive a truck through, well, a truck that was shrunken down like they were. The opening was covered with sticks, dirt and rocks all the way to the top. Yuma walked up to the pile of debris and called out an Indian word. The debris began to move out toward them.

Jimmy started to run back the way he came, but Yuma stopped him. "They open door."

"Who open door? I mean, who's opening what door and where does it lead?" Jimmy sputtered.

The debris door was transported by a cart-like object. It slowly moved forward and came to a stop, leaving them enough room to get in beside it. Jimmy noticed that the front looked like an old metal fly container that his grandfather John Farrell used for storing fly fishing hooks. The metal was supported by a couple of thick sticks, and fishing line held it all together. The whole setup was on a couple of wheels that came off a toy car, and the sticks and rocks on the front were held in place by clay and string.

"Trust me," Yuma said, and Jimmy didn't see that he had any option. He followed with small, hesitant steps, looking around at everything in all directions. As they walked through the opening two older Indian men, dressed the same as Yuma, spoke a greeting which Jimmy didn't understand.

The light source was a shaft that came in from a crack in the wall. It illuminated just enough that the men could see what they were doing as they rolled the door back into place. Once it was closed, they took the two ropes fastened on either side of the door and wrapped them around a giant nail wedged into a crack on the floor. Yuma spoke to them in their language as he handed them the strap from his horse. They nodded their heads in agreement and went down the inside path in a hurry.

"What did you tell them? Yuma, did you ask if Tommy was here?"

"No, I told them to go get so-ga. I think friend is here, I saw footsteps of braves at river."

They continued down the path through a crack in the slate. The shaft of light at the entrance gave out before long, and then they went into darkness. The air was damp and musty, and Jimmy could hear dogs at the end of the tunnel.

It's like walking in a cave without a flashlight. Jimmy felt the walls to make his way forward. After a while, he could see light again. At the end of the path, the light was so bright that Jimmy thought that they were going back outside. Up ahead he could see some kind of building where two small dogs were tied.

What is that? It looks like a cabin, he thought.

The path became wider and they entered a huge hollowed-out area in the middle of the slate mountain. In front of Jimmy was a whole Indian village with dozens of huts made up of sticks, pieces of bark and metal containers that were once candy boxes. The roof on one hut looked like an opened hard book cover. All were bound with an assortment of string, fishing line and clay—things found around the area and put to good use.

Jimmy took it all in with amazement. Then it sank in. "Wow. This is really happening. I shrank, and now I'm in a real live Indian village, the Takoda Indians. I can't wait to tell Jo that it's all true." Jimmy was captivated by this timeless marvel before him. "Wait till I bring him here, he's going to freak."

CHAPTER 4

THE HIDDEN VILLAGE

Jimmy could tell by the age of the items used in constructing the buildings that the village had continued growing over time. The oldest huts were made of stones. The next set had tin, the kind used to package foods like candy and peanuts, turned upside down with doorways cut out of the sides. In the next area, most of the roofs were made of book covers, and the walls were made out of wood scraps, like pieces of an old wagon or picture frames. The newest group of huts incorporated plastic in their design.

"It's like a living time line that keeps growing," Jimmy said to himself, grinning a little.

He looked past the huts to the rest of the village with cows, chickens, pigs, gardens, trees and of course the dogs. Right in the middle of it all was a pond, a pretty big one.

There was so much light in there that Jimmy thought he was outside until he looked up and noticed a slate ceiling with a big mirror in the middle of it.

"Wow. This is great, but how do you get so much light in here?" Jimmy asked Yuma, who was still standing by his side.

"Come, Plain Old Jimmy, I will show you."

Yuma led Jimmy to the end of one wall, the highest part of the huge cave, and pointed to a series of hand mirrors set on different angles which reflected light down from an opening at the top of the mountain. The last mirror was in the middle of the ceiling and reflected light down to the ground. Jimmy looked up in amazement at the way it was distributing light to the whole village.

An Indian girl close to Jimmy's age appeared and spoke to Yuma in their native tongue.

The chief turned to Jimmy. "This is Aponi, daughter of Yuma".

Jimmy cleared his throat as he looked at the beautiful young Indian girl. She was dressed in traditional clothes, complete with fringe, and her hair in a ponytail bound by a ribbon of leather.

"What's your name again?" Jimmy stammered.

"My name is ah-PAH-nee," Aponi said.

"Aponi. That's a real nice name. Does it mean anything?" Jimmy asked with a smile on his blushing face.

Aponi stepped up before her father could answer. She bowed her head a little, looking up at Jimmy, and spoke in the softest voice he had ever heard. "Aponi means butterfly. Do you know butterfly?"

"Yes. I have a collection of butterflies in my room." His blush turned to red embarrassment. He wanted to hide his face but could not turn away.

"What is your name?" Aponi asked, returning the smile.

"He is Plain Old Jimmy," Yuma answered.

"No, my name is Jimmy. When I told you my name before, I didn't mean to say that. I meant to say—aw, just forget it."

"Okay, Plain Old Jimmy, I will forget. Your friend is here. Aponi told me he is with medicine man."

"He's with the medicine man?" Jimmy said with concern in his voice. "Why? What's wrong with him? Is he all right?"

Yuma spoke with Aponi again in their language, then said to Jimmy, "I do not know. You go with Aponi now, she will take you to friend."

Aponi led him to one of the older huts, decorated with all kinds of feathers and colorful wall paintings. He went inside and saw Tommy asleep on a cot. He was a little banged up, but his wounds had been cleaned and dressed.

Jimmy knelt down by his side. "Hey, Tommy. Wake up. It's me, Jimmy."

Tommy did not respond.

"What's wrong with him? Why doesn't he wake up?"

Aponi said a few words to the medicine man in their language, and he answered.

She knelt down next to Jimmy and took his hand in hers. "Your friend has the sleeping sickness, he might sleep for a long time."

Jimmy leapt to his feet. "Sleeping sickness! What's that? He doesn't have any sleeping sickness. He's just tired, he's been through a lot."

"Maybe," Aponi said hesitantly. "I hope you are right. You have been through a lot, also. You should rest for a little bit. I will call you when your friend wakes up. There is nothing you can do for him now. Come with me."

Aponi took him to a hut close by, where she made up a cot for him. From a woven reed basket in the corner of the room, she selected pants and a vest made out of animal pelts and strips of leather. Next to the basket was a pair of moccasins, and she put them with the clothing beside the cot.

"You should change from your wet clothes before you get sick.

Here are some things that you can wear to keep warm." She left the hut, untying the flap to give him privacy.

He changed into the dry clothes thinking how much had happened since he lost Tommy in the stream. Lying on the cot, he realized this was the first chance he had to ponder the situation. He tossed and turned, too jittery to sleep with concern for Tommy taking over his mind, so he got up and went out to look around.

He was amazed at the wonderful village, which seemed to be right out of a Western. Except the houses were only about five or six inches tall, and the big wash bowl in Jimmy's hut was made from half of a ping pong ball. The hut was one of those with the wooden walls, and the ceiling was made out of a couple of big playing cards, with the three-of-diamonds right in the middle.

He walked to where some kids were playing a game like hockey, hitting a stuffed leather ball with sticks. The only thing different was there weren't any nets.

"I guess there aren't any winners, or any losers," he said to himself as he turned and continued investigating more of this marvel of nature. He checked out the pond where kids were swimming around. A spring right next to the pond kept feeding fresh water into it. A woman came and filled what looked like a ceramic thimble with water from the spring. On the other side of the pond, the water ran out and down a stream that ran through the town to a crack in the ground. He saw the spot where he and Chief Yuma had entered. He went over just in time to meet the two men who had opened the door for him and Yuma when they arrived. They were leading two other men who were pulling a cart.

"You are Plain Old Jimmy, yes?"

Jimmy opened his mouth to explain the name again, but decided against it and just nodded.

"I am Akando, and this is Anoki. We go to where Yuma say that you have fight with so-ga, we bring back for food." Just as he said that, the others passed Jimmy and he could see what was on the cart. It was the crawfish that Yuma had shot with the bow and arrow. Jimmy had a quick flashback and trembled uncontrollably for a few seconds.

"So, Akando, I guess so-ga means crawfish, or giant crawfish?"

"Yes." Akando answered but was immediately interrupted by a sweet, familiar voice.

"Just crawfish or lobster, not giant," Aponi said as she walked up.

"Oh, hi, Aponi. I wasn't really getting any rest, you know. This is a lot for me to take in. The whole thing with Tommy, the Red Ring flower, the shrinking, and the crawfish, my mind is spinning out of control. So I figured that I would take a look around. Is that okay?"

Aponi smiled at him. "You can look around all that you like, Jimmy. Would you like me to take you on a tour?"

His face lit up like it was Christmas. "Sure, that would be great."

She took Jimmy by the hand, and he at once blushed again. Aponi looked at Jimmy as he turned his head, hiding his red face. She let out a giggle and led him down the path back into the village. As they walked, Aponi turned to Jimmy with a curious look on her face.

"Can you tell me about this Magic Red Ring you spoke of? You know, the shrinking? I have heard my father and Anoki talk of this before."

Jimmy let out a giggle himself. "Tell you? It was your ancestors who made it. You should know more about it than I do. I just found out about the whole thing a day or two ago, you have lived it your whole life."

She stopped and led him to the side where she sat down on a rock, pulling him next to her. "What do you mean lived it my whole life? What should I know more than you? I know very little about the Magic Red Ring. Women and children are forbidden to talk of such things. I only know what I hear the braves talking about, but they become silent when they see that I am listening. I know the magic was created by one of the ancient medicine men to protect the tribe, but that is it.

And what do you mean about the shrinking?" She looked at him with a need for explanation in her eyes.

"You mean you really don't know anything at all, but what you told me? Aponi, there is so much more, the story goes on forever. I have to ask you something first. Why do you speak such good English while your father, Akando and Anoki speak like they are just starting to learn it?"

"What is English?" she asked.

"It's the name of the language we are speaking now. How did your people learn it, and how come you speak it better than anybody else I've met?"

"We call it the tongue of the visitors. One day, long before I was born, a man and woman came to the village and said that we will need to know this language some day."

Jimmy interrupted her. "What visitors? Is there someone else here from my world? Maybe he can help Tommy?"

Aponi put a finger over his lips. "There is no one else from your world here, not any more. They have been gone from your world for many, many years. They came long before my grandfather's father was born. Their children's children are part of the tribe now. We teach the language from generation to generation, in the school that the visitors made for us. I love these words, so I practice reading and writing a lot. Most of the others learn enough to communicate in the language, but as they get older, they use it less and less. Come, I will show you the school."

Once again she grabbed Jimmy by the hand and led him down the path.

"So, tell me about your tribe, Aponi. What kind of Indians are Takoda? I've never heard of that tribe before."

Aponi answered him in a proud tone. "The tribe was started from the Abenaki, but now there are men and women from many different tribes here. We are made up of all the Indians that chose peaceful ways. We hold our lives, and the lives of others, precious. There were also a lot of men and women from your world that joined us, you know, white men. They too desired peace. Since we were not any one individual tribe, we called ourselves by the life we lead. That is why we call ourselves Takoda, which means Friend to all."

"I know an Abenaki Indian," Jimmy said. "He lives next door to me. He's the one who told me about the Magic Red Ring flower."

Aponi became very excited. "Please, Jimmy. Tell me about this Red Ring flower now, please."

"Okay, but I don't think that you're going to believe me."

Jimmy told her everything Jo-Pac had told him, plus all that had happened to him and Tommy. She gazed at him, seemingly fascinated by what he was saying. He knew that she was reluctant to believe his story by her expression. "I know it's hard to believe, but it's the truth. Look at that crawfish. Have you ever seen one that big?"

Aponi looked at him in frustration. "Do they come any smaller? I have never seen a so-ga, I mean a crawfish, smaller than that."

Jimmy could tell that she had never seen much more than this village. "Look, Aponi, I wouldn't lie to you. There is another world out there, a very large and dangerous world, and when I say large and dangerous, I mean it in every way."

Then he pointed out a few of the things that were obvious to him, like the three-of-diamonds, the half ping pong ball and the shelter that was ahead of them made out of a saddlebag. "And what about the sunlight, Aponi? Why do you think you need all of the mirrors instead of being right outside?"

Aponi stopped him right in front of the saddlebag. "They say it is too dangerous out in the wild for women and children. There is glass on the top, past all the mirrors, to block the wild animals and snakes from entering. A long time ago, before the glass wall, a snake got in here and killed many braves before they could stop it. Ever since the glass wall was put up, we have been much safer."

"That's just it, Aponi, in the real world, the only snake you have to fear is a poisonous one. You don't need all that stuff like a glass wall or a mountain to protect your village from animals, because we are the ones that all the animals fear. They don't come into our villages, well not too often, and most of the time it's only when they are really hungry."

He could see in her face that in some way he was beginning to reach her. She looked around, as if she didn't want to draw attention to the two of them. "Come in here, this is the school."

She led him into the giant saddlebag and over to a pile of books, shrunken most likely by some persons who had them when they shrank, like Tommy's knife. Aponi dug deep into one of the piles behind everything else. She pulled a children's story book out from its hiding spot, and opened the cover to a page from another book.

"I had a complete book like this one, but my father took it away from me. He said that this book would scare the children, so he burned it. This is all that is left," she said as she extended the single page to him. It was a picture of a boy about to step on a snake, and it looked like it came from an old wildlife magazine.

"They told me that this was a very dangerous giant, and there were many more beyond the great river. That is why we are never allowed to go into the woods anymore. My father used to take me outside the mountain sometimes to show me the beautiful river and the sunshine, but that was a long time ago. Only the braves go out there now, they say it is not safe for women and children anymore." Gently she took the page back and put it in its hiding place.

She looked right into Jimmy's eyes. "One time, long ago, I snuck out and went for a ride on my horse along the river to a place where I saw one of these giant boys. He was sitting on top of a great cliff, fishing in the river where the water becomes calm like a giant pond. The boy looked so peaceful, I wished that I could have talked with him. For the longest time I thought that it was all a dream. Well, that is what my father said it was, and it was much easier to believe him than what

I thought I saw. When I met you today, I knew that it wasn't a dream. The boy I saw that day was you. You looked so peaceful I knew you could never harm anybody, you could not be a mean giant. When I saw you with my father today I thought the spirits brought you to me, the peaceful boy I had wanted to talk with, that time by the river."

Jimmy responded excitedly. "That's it. That's where Tommy fell into the stream, that's where we fish all the time."

At the thought of Tommy, he lost his smile and put his head down. "I hope he's going to be all right. We should go check on him."

When they got back to the medicine man's hut, Tommy was still unconscious. All his wet clothes were off except his shorts. The medicine man was marking Tommy with painted stripes up and down his arms, legs, chest, and face. Aponi said he was helping Tommy and that he had helped two out of the five braves with sleeping sickness.

"Only two. What happened to the other three?" Jimmy cried out.

Aponi looked at Jimmy and shook her head implying that they never woke up.

"What?" Jimmy shouted. "There is no way Tommy is going to die here. I have to get him some help." Jimmy stormed out of the medicine man's hut and headed for the entrance of the village. Aponi dashed after him.

"Wait. Jimmy, wait! You cannot go out there alone. Even if you get past the braves, the dogs will let them know that you are there. And if you do get past them, you'll still be in great danger out there."

"No, I won't. Remember, I'm the giant. I am going to get some help for my friend."

"But you are still too young. You will have to wait until you are a man. That is what I heard my father say to my mother, you are going to have to live here now."

He interrupted, "No way! I can't live here. I live with my parents, and they're going to expect me home in a couple of days. I haven't even checked in with them since we started out yesterday. You know, they might worry and come looking for me. And Tommy, what about Tommy? We have to get him to a doctor. He can't stay here in his condition."

"I am sorry," Aponi said. "I wish I could help."

Jimmy stepped up to her. "You can help. You can tell me how to get to the place where you saw me fishing. I'll eat a Red Ring flower bulb and go get a doctor for Tommy."

Aponi turned away from him and walked a few steps ahead. Jimmy caught up with her and gently grabbed onto her arm. He turned her around so she was facing him.

"Please, Aponi. Help me or my friend might die."

"Do you understand? If what they say about the giants of your world is true and you brought one back, it could put my people in danger of what the elders were trying to protect us from. Anyway, we would never be able to get him past everybody."

Jimmy interrupted again. "I have an idea. What if I bring Jo back here? He's a good man who would never tell anybody about this place. Jo would know what to do. Please, Aponi. It's the only chance Tommy has," he said with a feeling of hopelessness.

Aponi put her head down. And after a minute or two, she lifted her head and looked at Jimmy. "Okay, I will help, but you must take me with you. I want to see your world."

Jimmy was so excited that he wrapped his arms around her and gave her a hug. As soon as he realized what he had done, his red cheeks were back again.

"Come on, let's go." He reached for her hand, starting to lead her away.

She pulled her hand back. "No. Wait. Not now, they will stop us before we get to the river. Besides, it will be dark soon, and it is very dangerous out there at night. Not even the best braves leave the village at night. After the meal tonight we must go to sleep early. We will wake up before anybody else tomorrow and be at the entrance before the sun comes out. That is the only time we can sneak out and have enough time to make it there."

Jimmy thought it over, and then asked, "What about the dogs?"

"I am the one who takes care of the dogs, they don't bark at me."

They started back toward the center of town. Jimmy saw a great fire over which a group of women were cooking the monstrous crawfish. Another group of women were preparing corn, greens and about a dozen other food items Jimmy didn't recognize.

"Wow. This is cool. All of you eat together? It's like a big family cookout, an enormous family cookout."

Aponi smiled and nodded. "We are one big family."

During the meal, Jimmy sat between Yuma and Aponi. As they were eating, members of the tribe came over to welcome Jimmy, offering their sympathy and good thoughts for his friend's speedy recovery. Some of them just wanted to try out their English on an outsider. They were all very nice to Jimmy and he thought, "If only Tommy were awake, this would be so much more fun."

Yuma asked Jimmy a few questions about how he was feeling after a very long day, and if he liked his meal. Jimmy was curious as to why none of the braves asked about the Magic Red Ring flower. It seemed strange that he was just in from the world that they originally had come from, and they weren't interested.

After the meal, Yuma asked Jimmy to walk with him.

"Plain Old Jimmy, you must keep silent about Magic Red Ring. My people would not understand your world, it is not good for them. We no longer belong in your giant world, we are peaceful people and if go to the world of today, many of my people will get very scared, even die in this world they do not understand. I know of your world from my father, Jolon. He went with his father when he was young to get supplies to repair our home. One day a great storm came and washed away all of the Red Ring flowers and moved the river and earth all around. He and his father Chief Paco searched for many years to find the Red Ring flower, and they never found flower. One day, many years later when I was a little boy, my father found Red Ring flower once again, and he told Chief Paco the good news. Chief Paco say to go and see the world which they were not part of for so many years. Before he leave, my father tell me if he does not return, giant world is a bad place and no one must ever go there again. He did not return. So do you understand, Plain Old Jimmy, why my people must not know?"

Jimmy nodded and replied, "I can see how you would worry about your people in a world that they have never seen before."

Jimmy thought about what Yuma had said. "That storm must have been the big one my grandfather told me about, that happened more than fifty years ago. It moved the stream about twenty feet, and there were mudslides all over the place. So, how long ago did your father leave?"

Yuma answered with sadness in his voice, "Father has been gone thirty-three years."

"It is a different world out there now, Yuma, but it is my world and I belong there. Aponi said that you won't let me leave, but I promise that if you do I won't tell anybody about this place."

Yuma put his hand on Jimmy's shoulder and shook his head. "I am sorry, Plain Old Jimmy, maybe in time when you understand our people more, but not now."

Jimmy, knowing that he and Aponi had a totally different plan, didn't argue.

They walked back to where Aponi was sitting, and Yuma told her to help Jimmy settle in. Yuma told Jimmy to sleep well, as did all of his new friends, and Aponi led him to the hut with the three-of-diamonds in the center of the ceiling.

As he was about to go in, he whispered to her, "When are we going to leave?"

"Very early tomorrow morning," she whispered back. "Before anyone wakes up. I will come and get you, but we must be very careful not to wake anybody. Then we will get the horses and ride to your fishing place." She said good night, then turned and walked to her own hut.

Jimmy went into the hut and put the flap down, covering the doorway. He lay on his cot impatiently, waiting for Aponi to return for him. All he could think about was Tommy, and if he was going to be able to help him in time. He changed to his own clothes, so he wouldn't attract any attention if he ran into his parents when he got back. He checked his pockets to see if the lighter was still there, and it was. He was really wishing for his pocketknife, or Tommy's. He had no idea where they put Tommy's knife, or if he lost it when he fell in the water.

After a few hours of sleep, Aponi opened the flap and walked silently into his hut. "Are you ready, Jimmy?" she whispered.

"Ready?" he answered as he woke up and sprung to his feet. "I can't wait, let's get going."

Aponi led him into the darkness, moving slowly and quietly. Everyone else in the village was asleep.

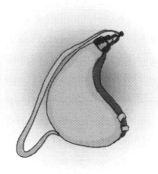

CHAPTER 5

GOING FOR HELP

*A*poni went ahead of Jimmy to greet the three dogs that were tied to a fence surrounding a large building near the entrance of the village. The building, made from scraps of wood and book covers, was used as a barn.

When the dogs were calm enough to keep quiet, she called Jimmy over. "We keep them here to warn us if a predator comes through the tunnel. They bark, and that gives the braves a good chance to defend us."

She sent Jimmy to the entrance of the tunnel in between the layers of slate. "You wait there," she said before disappearing into the large building.

Shortly, she returned leading two palomino horses that were smaller than the chestnut he had ridden with Yuma yesterday. She handed

Jimmy the end of the leather string tied around the neck of one of the horses. The horse had a small, colorful blanket on its back.

"What about the saddle, Aponi? I can't ride without a saddle."

Without a word, she headed back to the stable with the other horse.

"Aponi, where are you going?"

"You said that you can't ride like this, so we will only take one horse. I will guide the horse, and you ride on back holding on to me."

That suited Jimmy just fine. "Jackpot," he said to himself.

She returned and handed him a suede leather pouch with some arrows and a bow tucked into it and leather canteens tied to the strap.

"You can carry this," she said as they headed through the wide crack in the slate.

The tunnel was dark even in the daytime, but now there was no shaft of light at the end. Aponi appeared to know her way. She led the horse and Jimmy followed the sound of the walking horse, or the smell. He couldn't decide which.

Once they got to the door of sticks and rocks, she felt around on the ground looking for the ropes fastened to the ground holding the rolling door in place. He reached into his pocket, pulled out his lighter and turned the little wheel that lit it. She stared at the fire that came from his hand.

"What is that, Jimmy? How did you make fire come from your hand?"

She must be used to making fire by rubbing two sticks together or something like that, he thought.

"It's called a lighter. There are all different kinds. I take it camping with me for my fires."

She looked closer at the lighter. "Wonderful, but is this the only fire you know how to make?"

"That's it. If this breaks when I'm in the woods camping, I go cold and hungry unless I have blankets and food that doesn't have to be cooked. I learned how to make fire with sticks in the boy scouts, but I wasn't very good at it."

She gave him a gentle pat on the back. "I will teach you how to make fire very good, so you are never cold and hungry."

She laughed as they both finished untying the rope and pushed the door forward. They went through the opening and could see the sun was about to peek above the mountain.

"I love the way the sun wakes up in the morning. I used to come out here to greet the sun a lot with my father. But one day my father said that it was too dangerous for me to come out here anymore. He said there were giant dogs that would hurt me."

"Hurt you? Aponi, your father was talking about Horace Phlegmats' attack dogs, Satan and Lucifer. They would kill you."

"They almost did. That was the day I saw you, the last time I was ever allowed outside in the wild."

Jimmy thought about that while they watched the sunrise. He was experiencing it from a completely new angle. That day the sun appeared ten times larger, like everything else around him. The tall grass around the slate mountain looked like tropical trees, and he was so close to the ground that he could smell the dew on their blades.

In the sunlight, he could see that Aponi was dressed differently. Today she wore traditional fringed leather pants and moccasins but with a long tunic of tan linen-like fabric. *Maybe from one of the English-speaking visitors.*

Aponi broke the silence. "We have to leave; the braves will get up soon and come out to hunt."

They rolled the door back into place. Aponi leapt up on the horse. Jimmy jumped up two or three times, refusing the hand she offered him. Finally he gave up and let her help as he pulled himself onto the back of the horse.

They went down the slate mountain straight into the woods, coming out along the stream. Aponi guided the horse upstream along the same path Jimmy was on yesterday with her father. They rode hard.

This time Jimmy kept his eyes open. He wanted to know the location of the slate mountain so that when he was big again he might help the villagers out once in a while. But the world was just too big for him to make sense of. There were some familiar spots and some that totally confused him.

"I can't get a grasp on where we are, Aponi. I thought that I knew these woods like the back of my hand."

After several minutes of uncertainty, they came to a small bridge— that is, small in the giant way. He recognized this bridge as the one crossing the stream behind his house.

"I know where we are. This is the tractor bridge along our property line that leads back to Phlegmats' domain. Once we pass the bridge, we'll be in safe territory."

They continued along the path under the bridge. A splash surprised him, the sound intensified to his small ears. He caught sight of it in mid-air, the biggest trout he had ever seen.

"It's a whale," Jimmy said. "I guess you see trout like that all the time, don't you?"

She didn't answer.

"Aponi, don't you?"

She was frozen, with her eyes fixed on the stream. "What was that?"

A confused Jimmy asked, "What do you mean, what was that? Don't you see fish that size all the time?"

She shook her head. "I have never seen a fish that big; it could eat my horse in one or two bites. The fish that the braves bring back must be babies. We have fish in our pond, but they are much smaller. I guess the elders shrank them down too, the pond is filled with them."

She leaned forward and started to ride again. When they reached the other side of the bridge, she said, "We have to stop for a little bit. We need to give Nodin a rest and some water."

"Is that the horse's name—Nodin?"

"Yes, it means wind. That is the way she runs, like the wind."

They stopped by the stream, using a low branch for cover. Aponi patted the horse on the back, and let her go to drink. Then Aponi and Jimmy took the leather canteens to the stream, filled them with water and sat down on a rock to rest.

After a few minutes, she stood and announced it was time to go. He stretched, trying to walk off the pain his backside felt from the hard ride.

"Boy," he said. "My butt didn't feel this sore yesterday. I guess there was too much going on to notice."

Something caught his eye, and he dashed over to the stream and reached down to the ground.

"Hey, this is my gear bag that fell off the other day when I jumped into the water after Tommy. I guess the current took it down here. We better hang on to this, we might be able to use this stuff later." He tucked it into the pouch with the bow and arrows.

Aponi jumped onto the horse and extended her hand once more.

"Pride goeth before the fall," he said as he took her hand. "And my butt is hurting enough, I don't need another fall."

Yuma had just heard that the door to the village was not tied from the inside and Aponi's horse was missing. He ran to the entrance to see for himself. As he made his way through the tunnel, one of his braves ran up to him.

"We cannot find Aponi. We think Aponi went with Plain Old Jimmy. He is not in his shelter, and he has taken his clothes."

Yuma sent the brave back to the village to bring more braves and, when they were assembled, sent them out to search for the two children. He watched as the men rode off up the river.

"Aponi," he whispered into the world outside the tunnel. "Where are you?"

CHAPTER 6

OBSTACLES ALONG THE WAY

$\mathcal{A}$poni and Jimmy had been riding for a while when she abruptly halted the horse. She quickly guided Nodin into the brush.

"What's the matter, Aponi? Why did we stop?"

She put a finger to her lips. "SHHH! Look over there, we will not be able to travel past them."

He pushed aside leaves blocking the view and peeked out. Two raccoons were turning rocks over one by one, looking underneath for living creatures that might be good eating like crawfish or tadpoles.

Jimmy panicked. "We're dead. A crawfish was going to eat me, imagine how fast those two will eat both of us, and Nodin too."

Aponi put her hands on the sides of his face and turned his head so that they were facing each other. "Calm down, they will not eat us if they do not see us." She covered his mouth with her hand. "Or hear us. They will not smell us, we are downwind of them."

She slowly took her hand away from his mouth, and he was quiet so she took her hand away completely. She threw her leg up over Nodin's head and slid noiselessly down the horse's back. As Jimmy began to slide off, he lost his grip and tumbled down off the horse, rolling right down the embankment to the side of the stream.

The two raccoons looked through their black masks toward the sound. Aponi motioned down to him to be still as she took out the bow and two arrows from the pouch. She aimed high into the red oak trees above the raccoons and shot. Two seconds later an acorn dropped on pebbles behind the raccoons, making a rattling noise on the gravel. The scared raccoons ran upstream and into a tree.

"Great shot!" Jimmy yelled, watching the striped tails disappear into the woods. "Way to go!"

Aponi tied Nodin to a bush and hurried down to Jimmy. "I am lucky, not a great shot. Are you okay? Did you get hurt?"

Rubbing his backside as he stood up, he admitted, "This trip is beating the heck out of me. How do the braves in your village do this every day?"

She laughed as she put her arm around him and lifted his arm over her shoulder to support him. Leading him back up the embankment, she said, "The body feels the way the mind tells it to feel. All you have to do is stop telling your body to say ouch."

They made their way back up the embankment. Jimmy thought it would be easier for him to help her up, so this time he attempted to climb on the horse first. Aponi untied the horse and held her steady while Jimmy maneuvered from the top of a rock.

He whispered into the horse's ear as he prepared to climb on, "Okay, Nodin, please don't make me look like a complete geek. I promise that if you let me do this and keep my dignity, I will bring you back some sugar cubes from home."

All at once Nodin bolted, leaving Jimmy airborne. Aponi, still holding the pouch with all their gear, was knocked to the ground by the bucking horse.

Nodin ran off in the direction of the village, not even slowing down or looking back for a second.

"What's the matter? Doesn't your horse like sugar? All horses like sugar," Jimmy said as he climbed to his feet, watching the horse disappeared into the distant woods.

"Well, I guess we are on our own," Aponi declared as Jimmy helped her up.

He looked to her in astonishment. "Are you kidding? What are we going to do on our own, except maybe die?"

"This is what I meant before when I said the body feels the way the mind tells it to feel. You are giving up before we have even started. Why are you so worried about our trip? This is a land you have traveled many times. The only thing that is different this time is that you are smaller."

He put his head up and looked upstream, trying to be as strong as he thought Aponi was. "You're right. I promise that I am going to stop being so negative." With those words, he took a step on some loose gravel and slid down right into the water.

"I am glad you are going to stop being, as you said, negative, or you might get mad instead of seeing this as a sign to refill the canteens that Nodin knocked over."

He grinned and, without another word, limped over to where the canteens were and picked them up off of the ground. He walked back down, filled the canteens and walked back up to Aponi.

She patted him on the back and grabbed one of the canteens for a drink. "You should have stayed where you were. The path is that way," she said with a big smile on her face, as she pointed toward the stream.

They went upstream again. Jimmy, knowing he had to be a

gentleman no matter what, carried the gear in one hand. With the other, he held his backside. He was limping, and every few steps he let out a moan.

Aponi laughed and apologized, and laughed again.

It took a long time get anywhere, taking steps a fraction of the length they used to be. It seemed like they walked forever, but it was only late morning when Jimmy saw something familiar. "That's where your father found me about to be eaten by the crawfish. We're getting closer to the fishing pool, it won't be much longer. Should we stop and take a rest and get some fresh water?"

"Okay. Do you want me to get some soft grass for you to sit on?" she asked, still laughing. He stood up after refilling the canteens and rubbed his backside once more.

"No, that's okay. I'm feeling much better now. Here, have some. It's nice and cold," he said as he passed her the canteen.

"Thank you. I can use a cool drink."

Jimmy sat next to her and, to take his mind off the aching, picked up a stone smaller than a grain of rice. He tossed it into the stream and watched the small ripples it made. Then he threw another stone into the ripples.

"What are you doing?" Aponi asked.

"Oh, it's a game called ripple stone that we play at scout camp. What kind of games do you play in your village?"

Aponi threw a small stone and watched the ripples. While reaching for another stone, she said, "We play all kinds of games, like cat's cradle. You take a piece of string..."

Jimmy interrupted, "I used to play that when I was younger."

Aponi continued, "And we play little pines, where we tie little pieces of straw in a cluster and place them on a board. Two or three of us each take a side of the board, and shake it. This makes the little pines dance."

"Who wins that game?"

"There is no winner. If games have a winner, then they have a loser, too. In this game, we are all happy at the end. We also make dolls out of straw and material, and sometimes we make little homes for them."

"Do the boys have their own games, or do they play the same games as the girls?"

She swatted at him. "Of course boys have their own games, most of the games the young braves play have winners and losers. They have contests with their bows and arrows, the closest to the center wins. They also play canoe tipping. A few boys stand in a canoe and rock it. The last one on the canoe who doesn't fall in the water is the winner. This is their favorite game."

"Hey, that's like king of the mountain. I play that all the time, and I'm the best. What else, Aponi?"

"Well, they play a lot of spear, slingshot and fishing games which help them to become skillful with the tools and weapons that they will use as braves. What about the children in your world? What kinds of games do you play?"

Jimmy told her about some of the games that kids play like tag, hide and seek, and snake in the grass. He felt it was inappropriate to mention cowboys and Indians, so he left that out.

"What games do girls play?" Aponi asked.

"Well, I guess jump rope and maybe dolls."

"Dolls are my favorite thing to play."

"My all-time favorite thing is baseball," Jimmy said with excitement in his voice. I play in a little league, and I am very good. Last year my batting average was the highest on the team."

"What is batting average, Jimmy?"

She's lost. Never heard about baseball, the poor thing. "Here, I'll show you."

He looked around for a stick, picked one up about the length of a cotton swab and swung it a few times. "A little too long," he said and broke off about a third of it over his thigh. He swung the remainder and pronounced, "Just right." Near his feet were a few flat stones about half the size of BBs, he picked them up and stashed them in his pocket. "I'll show you why they call me 'Slugger.'"

He threw a stone into the air, grabbed onto the stick and prepared to swing. The stone came down, and he swung. "Strike one," he said as he dug in his pocket for another stone. The same thing happened twice more. "I guess I'm out of practice. Don't worry, I'll get it right."

Aponi looked puzzled. "What is supposed to happen?"

"Just wait. I'll show you." He bent back down and picked up a nice, big stone. He took a deep breath, and stretched his arms a little with the stick leaning against his legs as if at the plate.

Aponi started giggling.

Just as he was throwing the stone into the air, Aponi heard the two raccoons coming out of the brush. "Wait, don't do it."

It was too late. He swung, and it connected. "Look at that go!" he said, and the two of them watched it hit the first raccoon right in the nose.

This time the raccoons saw where the stone came from and they weren't scared away. They headed right for the two kids. Jimmy stared at them, unable to move a muscle.

"Come on!" Aponi screamed as she grabbed him, giving him a jump start. They ran under the closest big rock they could find along the stream.

The raccoons followed them right to the rock and started digging at where they went under. Luckily, the ground was pretty solid under the rock.

"I think we're safe in here, but we are going to have to stay in here for a little while," Aponi gasped.

"I don't know, Aponi. Raccoons are very persistent, especially when they are hungry. They might try to…"

He was cut off by the movement of the rock right above their heads.

Gravel started to pour in from the sides of the rock covering up their feet. They stepped quickly away from the falling dirt and pebbles.

"Come on, this way." He led Aponi through a hole in between two stones. As they went through, one of the raccoons overturned the rock, letting the whole area fill in with dirt and stones.

"That was close. I hope they give up. Are you okay?" Jimmy asked as he extended his hand into the darkness.

"I am all right. What about you?"

"I'm fine," he said with a "whew" in his voice knowing she was okay.

The sheet of slate above their heads began to move back and forth. Gravel fell in on them. The raccoon was pulling at the rock. Each time the raccoon grabbed at the slate, it loosened a bit more. The slate was pulled up a little at a time, and with each tug by the raccoon a little more sunlight came in.

"Look, Jimmy, over there. We can go in that hollow log."

Toward the bottom of the slate was a hollowed out log with a hole on the side. As he considered it, the slate was jerked up, and a piece of stone slipped down the side, preventing the piece of slate from coming all the way back down. They were now uncovered and visible in the bright light.

"That'll work," Jimmy said. "Let's go."

"Wait. What is that?" Jimmy turned just in time to duck the swing of a giant claw. A monstrous crawfish stood between him and the hollow log.

"We ate his brother last night," Jimmy said as he pushed Aponi behind the monster and toward the log. "Now it's payback time. Hurry, get in the hole, quick!"

Aponi crawled in and maneuvered to help Jimmy get in. He dove for the hole and landed a little short. She stretched her arm out trying to reach his hand, but he started to slide backwards.

"Oh, no! He's got me!"

The crawfish had grabbed one of his pant legs. Jimmy was being dragged backward, stretched out with his arms over his head trying to clutch anything solid. Aponi jumped out of the log, grabbed his hands and engaged in a tug of war with the crawfish.

"Hold on to my hands, Jimmy!"

Without warning, the sheet of slate was overturned. The raccoons were still working it, trying to get to the two snacks that had been hiding there. The larger raccoon latched on to the crawfish. The crawfish let Jimmy go. Aponi dragged him into the log.

Breathless, she said, "The raccoon saw us. He will return."

"He'll enjoy his appetizer first."

After devouring the crawfish, the raccoon came for Aponi and Jimmy. They moved deep inside the log, hugging the walls. The log rocked back and forth and upended with the hole facing straight up. Jimmy could see the raccoon peek in and start to dig. They both fell to the bottom and pressed themselves down as far as they could.

The paw came closer and closer. Finally the animal put all its effort into a lunge, and his claw grazed Aponi's face. She turned to the side pressing her face down but couldn't get any further away. Jimmy reached over and took the leather pouch from her. He opened his gear bag in the pouch and retrieved one of the hooks he had packed. He rose up on his knees and swung it like a baseball bat.

"Take that! You ugly pain in the neck."

Wham! The hook stuck right into the raccoon's paw. The raccoon withdrew with the hook sticking in him but was ready to try again when he was knocked away from the opening by the other raccoon.

"Oh, great. I thought he was gone," Jimmy whimpered. "Between the two of them, we don't stand a chance, unless they fight for so long that they forget about us."

The two raccoons wrestled. They pushed the log around as they brawled, moving closer and closer to the water. Then, with a big thud, one of the raccoons jumped on top of the other and pushed him and the log into the water.

"Uh oh! Looks like we're going for a rough ride! Hold on!" Jimmy shouted over the swooshing of the rough current.

The log took off downstream, thrashing as if struggling to stay afloat. Inside, Jimmy and Aponi tried, but the twisting was so forceful that they couldn't stand up to see where they were going. It was all they could do to hold on to the sides.

"What's going to happen to us now, Jimmy? Where does this river end?"

"We could end up riding in this log for quite some time. The stream goes on for about three or four miles before hitting the Delaware River. But there is no way we'll make it that far, something will stop us. I just hope that something stops us soon, or else we're going to have some serious hiking to do."

Just then the log was thrown out of the water, tumbled and came to a crashing halt, sending both of them slamming against the wall.

Jimmy caught his breath and shakily jumped to his feet. He seemed to be all right. His pants were torn where the crawfish had grabbed him. He had forgotten about the pain in the rump but didn't have any new pains. He took a few small steps to get stable and then rushed over to where Aponi was lying. Her eyes were closed, and there was a scratch on her face.

"Are you all right, are you hurt?" he asked gently.

She opened her eyes. "I'm okay, just a little sore. But look at your leg, you're cut from the crawfish. Come here and sit down. I will tend to that before it gets worse."

She sat up and lifted the hem of her tunic to her face and bit a few threads of the fabric. Pulling on that rip, she tore a strip of material off at the bottom where it was frayed.

"Jimmy, where are the canteens?"

"Well, there's one of them, but it looks empty. I don't see the other one, it's probably with the raccoons," he said as he looked around. "I'll go out and fill this one."

"No. You sit back down, and I will get the water." Aponi guided him to a spot where he might be comfortable, while keeping his cut leg from bumping against anything. She climbed out of the hole with the canteen in her hand.

Jimmy used the solitude to think about the last two days: the Red Ring flower, the first and second ride down the stream, the first and second crawfish, the village, and most of all, his good friend Tommy. Thinking about Tommy saddened him, but that gave him the courage to go on. And then there was Aponi, beautiful Aponi. Ever since they met, Jimmy stopped thinking about Betty Ann Phlegmats.

After a few minutes, he began to wonder what happened to her. "Hey, where is she? She should have been back by now," he muttered.

"Aponi, where are you?" he shouted as he began to push himself up.

She stuck her head in the log. "I told you to sit down and rest until I take care of your leg."

"Yes, nurse. You know, you're as bad as my mother, maybe even worse."

Aponi sat inside the log and smiled as she poured water from the canteen onto the piece of cloth from her tunic. "I think I will like your mother, she sounds like a good woman."

She cleaned his cut and rinsed the cloth out before wrapping it around the wound. "There you are, it is all better. Oh, I almost forgot," she said with a squeal of delight as she ran over to the hole that was the entrance to their log shelter.

She stepped out momentarily and returned carrying a leaf that held four of the biggest blueberries he had ever seen. "Look what I have for us."

"Oh, wow, would you look at those. They have to be the size of a melon, a dark blue melon." Then he thought for a second. "Well, I guess they're just the size of a blueberry. I keep forgetting we're only a couple of inches tall."

Aponi laid the leaf down and Jimmy picked up a berry. He tried to bite into it but the skin was too hard to pierce with his teeth.

"How do we eat this, if we can't get through the skin?"

Aponi laughed, and Jimmy noticed her nose crinkled up a little.

"I brought a knife. I thought we might need one," she said, taking a knife from the pouch and holding it out handle first. He took hold of the knife and stuck it into the blueberry, causing it to burst and splash him in the face with dark blue juice.

"Now that is a juicy blueberry," he declared as he cut a section of the skin away and held the berry out. "Here, help yourself."

"Thank you," she said, sticking her hand into the berry and pulling out a glob of what looked like the wiggly gelatin served as dessert at family reunions.

He put the berry down on the leaf and dug in. "This is great. I never tasted a blueberry this good, not in my whole life. This is how I'm going to eat them from now on, I'm going to peel away the skin and only eat the insides. It might take a while, but it will be worth it."

"You make me laugh, you are very funny, Jimmy. I am having such a good time with you. I wish…" She silently put her head down.

"What? What do you wish?"

"I wish we could always be friends, but I know that is not possible. We come from two different worlds. When you get help for your friend, you will go and not return."

"No way, Aponi. Aside from what happened to Tommy, this is the best time I have ever had. I will always be your friend. I will visit you and you can come and visit me. I like you, and I'm not the kind of friend who would forget." With a big grin, he leaned over and gave her a little nudge on the shoulder, as a buddy would do.

She stood up in front of him and smiled back. "Good, I'm glad to hear that, because I will never forget you."

Then she leaned over and gave Jimmy a kiss on the cheek. She stood back up, and Jimmy could feel his smile being replaced with shock. He was frozen, speechless, and red as a cherry.

Laughing once again, Aponi scooped out some of the blueberry gel and smeared it all over his face. "Here, I will change the red to blue."

He jumped up and grabbed some blueberry gunk, holding it up ready to retaliate.

"No, no. Wait, Jimmy. Please, don't." She made a slight bow as if surrendering unconditionally.

Or so he thought. As soon as he put the berry mess aside, she reached back into the fruit with both hands and pulled out enough goo to smear over his whole head.

Then she retreated to the other side of the log. "Oh, Jimmy, you are such a sweet boy," she said, but it didn't work. He began the bombardment, covering everything in the log, except Aponi, with blueberry.

Finally he got her with a glob, right in the face. That was Jimmy's last shot.

"Oh no," he said, running to her side. "I'm sorry, I didn't mean it."

Aponi put her hands down and exposed her smiling blue face. "Don't be sorry. That was fun! I would like to keep playing, but it is getting late. Should we start walking?"

"You're right. We have a long way to travel, and we don't even know where we are."

They climbed out of the log and cleaned all the berry juice off themselves. They packed up all their gear and a couple of blueberries for the trip.

Jimmy visually checked out the area. "Well, at least we are on the right side of the stream, we don't have to worry about getting across later. But one problem is that I have no idea where we are. It all looks kind of familiar, but in a weird way."

As he turned from side to side with his head up, a look of recognition came over his face.

"What is it?" Aponi asked. "Do you know where we are?"

He answered with confidence. "I know exactly where we are. There's old Phlegmats' corn silo. We're—oh no—we're on Phlegmats' domain. We need to get out of here before those two demon dogs get a whiff of us."

Franticly, he grabbed the pouch and led the way upstream. They could hear barking in the distance.

"Are those the demon dogs?" Aponi asked.

"That's them, Satan and Lucifer, the two meanest dogs on the face of the earth. I'm just glad they're far away, but we still have to move fast, just in case."

The barking stopped, but Jimmy and Aponi kept up the fast pace, making the best time they could on their small legs.

All at once the barking started again, and it seemed to be right on top of them. They looked all around but didn't see anything.

Jimmy guided her to a tree. "We need to get up very high, very fast." As he climbed, he said, "These trees are much easier to climb at this size." Scaling the bark was as easy as walking up steps.

Aponi was having a harder time of it. Her legs were not as large or strong as Jimmy's and kept slipping.

"Hurry, Aponi! They could reach us at any second."

The dogs were barking wildly. Jimmy shouted down, "They know we're here, Aponi. Climb faster! There they are! They're coming for us, climb faster!"

Jimmy reached the first limb and climbed on it. He held his hand out to Aponi and helped her onto the branch. The dogs were headed right for them, and Jimmy was not sure if they were high enough. Satan and Lucifer reached the tree and jumped fanatically up toward the branch. Aponi and Jimmy pressed against the limb. The dogs were jumping up a little too close for comfort.

Jimmy figured that Horace Phlegmats heard the dogs barking by now and knew by the sound of their bark that they had something. It wasn't long until Jimmy was proved right. Old Horace came their way on foot. Satan ran over to him. Lucifer stopped jumping but didn't leave his post.

"We have to get up there," Jimmy whispered and pointed up to where two limbs branched out of the tree leaving a hollow space in the center of the trunk.

Aponi started up the side of the tree first and made it to the hollowed space. In his haste, Jimmy's foot broke off a loose piece of bark. He stopped still. It fell down the side of the tree, hitting dry leaves on the ground and making a crunching noise. Lucifer, still standing by the tree, looked for the source of the sound, and saw Jimmy clinging up the tree trunk like a bug. The dog began to yap and jump hysterically, and Satan ran to join him.

Jimmy knew he had to move quickly and made it to cover just before Horace reached the tree. Jimmy and Aponi were both as deep in as they could go, but the space wasn't as deep as it was wide. Their heads stuck out, and they could see Horace looking up toward them.

There he was, standing there in his old torn-up overalls, his dirty jean jacket, and a pair of boots that were ripped open on the sides. His bald crown was surrounded by long, stringy gray and black hair. He was unshaven with quite a few teeth missing and a pair of glasses with only one lens which was dirty.

"He is scary looking, Jimmy. Are you sure we are okay in here?"

"I don't know. I don't think he saw us, so let's keep it that way." Jimmy motioned her to stoop down so their heads were hidden.

Horace stepped up to the tree. "What is it, my babies? Did you see something? Was it a squirrel? A chipmunk? What?"

He stuck two of his fingers in the space between the branches. Jimmy and Aponi backed into a corner, shaking.

"Maybe it's one of them damn little Injuns, what da ya think? We know they're there, don't we? Them town folks might thinks we's nuts, but we knows the truth my babies." Horace pressed his one lens up against the hole, looking in toward the two kids.

He backed up and took his glasses off. He licked the lens, as he undid his jacket and pulled at his shirt to wipe it off. "Darn glass, can't see a thing out of it. Now let's have a better look." He leaned in toward the hole again, this time with a clear lens.

Suddenly there was a flutter from one of the branches above. He jumped back and saw a couple of blackbirds fly away. The demon dogs took off after the low-flying birds. Horace went after them, yelling their names, and a few other things.

Aponi fell to her knees in tears. Jimmy knelt down next to her and put his arm around her. She hugged him and continued to cry.

"I have never been so scared, not of the fish or the raccoons, not even of rolling in a log on a river. He was a giant. A mean, scary giant."

"It is the reality of this world. I am sorry I took you so far from your home and family." Jimmy stood up and helped her to her feet.

As they climbed out of the hole and onto one of the smaller branches, Aponi looked far off. "I hope my father will understand my decision. He is probably sitting on top of the slate mountain worried for the safety of his daughter."

A chilling breeze came up the tree. She trembled and looked down to the ground. "I will not go back down there again, the dogs might come back." Tears rolled down her face, and she repeated, "They might come back."

Jimmy wiped her tears away with his hands. "We'll stay here for a while and make sure they're gone."

She sat with her eyes closed, knees up against her chest, holding on tightly, still shaking. She took several deep breaths until the shaking stopped. She looked over at Jimmy. "How is your wound?"

He shrugged his shoulders. "It's fine, I guess. I didn't even remember it was there."

"That is good," Aponi laughed, "I won't have to carry you then?"

Jimmy was glad to see her more relaxed and smiled as he plotted out a route in his mind, trying to figure out the best and fastest way without spending much time down on the ground. Aponi didn't want to go back down to walking on the ground with those two dogs and the scary old man on the prowl. Jimmy didn't want her doing anything she didn't want to do, but he didn't see that they had much of a choice.

Just as he was about to let her know the plan, another breeze came by and rattled all the branches around them. He heard a ruffling coming from above them. As he looked up, a big grin took over his face.

"We're not going to go back down to the ground," he said. "Not until we are safe anyway."

"What do you mean? Are we going to try moving from tree to tree?"

"No, we are going to fly back." He pointed to a kite stuck in the tree, a couple of branches from the top.

"What is that?" Aponi asked, looking up at this big, strange, colorful object.

"It's my kite, my beautiful kite, another one of the toys that we play with in my world. We are going to fix it up to be our own glider. I lost it last month when the string broke just as it got nice and high. All we have to do is make a few changes and, presto, it's a custom-built glider."

"We are going to fly like a bird on that?" Aponi questioned, "How is that possible?"

"It's very simple. The kite is made of plastic, a very light material. When it catches the wind, it's lifted up into the air. There is a tail on the back that keeps it straight, so you just hold the string and let the kite and the wind do the rest. Even if there's no wind, the kite won't fall straight down. It will glide down as long as it is guided straight, I think. And it should hold our weight. I used to tie toy soldiers to kites and fly them, and we're not much bigger than they were."

She didn't look convinced. "Are you sure this will work?"

He gave it a few seconds' more thought and then frowned. "Well, we can either try to fly or go back down to the ground and walk through Phlegmats' domain and chance seeing Satan and Lucifer again. I leave it up to you, Aponi."

She stood up and looked down at the ground and shivered. Then she looked up at the kite. "Yes!" She shouted. "I am sure it will work. It has to work."

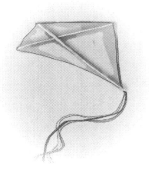

Chapter 7

High in the Sky

Jimmy and Aponi filled up on one of the stored blueberries to keep hunger away. They collected their gear and climbed higher into the tree, up to the branch Jimmy's kite was snagged on.

Jimmy got to work immediately. First he wriggled the kite until it was freed and let the breeze hold it in the air, tied to the branch by a string. He looped the end of the string up where the harness would be so that they could release it to become airborne.

He used Aponi's knife to cut away loose string from the end of the kite. "We'll use this as our harness to hold us up."

He looped string around the cross section of the wood that led to all four points of the kite. "There, that will be strong enough to hold both of us."

He tied fishing line from his gear bag to the tips of all four points and then joined them together in the middle. "We'll use these as our guide lines."

"What are guide lines for?" Aponi looked amazed at what he was doing, which made Jimmy feel really good.

"Simple," he said with confidence. "We're tied in to that harness, those two lines hanging from the middle of the kite. We hold on to the fishing line that is connected to the front, back and sides of the kite. When we want to turn left, all we do is pull the line from the left side of the kite. We do the same to turn right and pull the front string when we want to go down. We pull the back string when we feel a breeze to climb higher. And that ribbon on the end is our kite tail, it keeps us straight."

Aponi asked with a puzzled look on her face, "What about when we want to stop?"

He smiled proudly. "We just land like the hang gliders do, or we crash into high grass to break our fall."

"What about starting off? How do we start flying?"

"You see the string that is holding the kite up? Well, it leads to our harness. Once we're tied in, all we have to do is cut the string and we are headed out into the clear blue."

He checked the kite over and pulled on the lines to test them. He stood beside the aircraft and extended his hand to help her up. "Preflight inspection complete. Are you ready?"

She took his hand, and nodded. "Uh, yes, I think I am ready."

"All right. Let's go." He tied the gear bag to one of the harnesses, then Aponi, then himself. "Hold on tight!"

She held onto the harness with both hands, shutting her eyes.

"Here we go," he said, pushing off to make the kite swing out. It dangled in mid air a couple of inches away from the branch. He cut the line, and it dropped several inches but suddenly stopped.

"What is it, Jimmy? Are we stuck?"

"I don't know. Let's try to rock it loose."

The two of them leaned side to side in unison. They rocked for a few seconds, but it became apparent to Jimmy that nothing was going to happen.

"You stay here. I'm going to have to cut us loose from up there." He untied himself and climbed back onto the branch.

"Here it is. I see the problem. There's a knot in the line." He threw the line he had just cut down to Aponi. "Here, hold onto this and don't let go." He reached down and took the knife back out of the bag trying to cut away a piece of the branch so the line could slip through with the knot.

As he began cutting away at the last piece of branch that was holding the line back, he yelled down to Aponi, "Okay, I'm going to get it through soon, hold that line tight."

But before she could tighten her grip, the kite started to pull away, ripping it out of her hand. The kite dropped. Jimmy put the knife through his belt and grabbed the line as it slipped through the branch. The force was too strong for him, and down the line went, dragging Jimmy along the branch. He steadied himself by placing his foot in a crack on the branch and tried to pull the kite back. The kite was stronger, and Jimmy lost his footing.

A sudden gust of wind lifted the kite free from the branch and carried it above the tree, with Jimmy hanging on to the line. Jimmy's weight was pulling down on the one side. The kite was out of control.

Aponi reached out to him but her arms didn't stretch that far. "Swing back and forth until you are close enough for me to grab," she shouted.

He hunched up his knees and kicked to push himself backward and then forward. With each swing he got a little closer but not enough to reach her.

"Jimmy, your harness is close enough. Let go with one hand and grab your harness."

"I can't do it, Aponi, I don't have the strength." His hands slipped, and he fell farther down the on line.

"You can so do it!" she said sternly. "You have to! Remember, the body feels the way the mind tells it to feel. Tell your body that you can do it."

With the kite spinning around, Jimmy started to swing again. He said to himself over and over, "I can do it." His grip started to loosen, and he knew he had to do something so he lifted one of his legs and threw it over the string harness. Aponi grabbed onto his other leg. His hands lost hold of the line, and he dangled upside down with one leg in the harness and Aponi clutching the other.

It looked impossible. He thought he was a goner, then Aponi urged him to pull his body up, and he doubled over until his hand reached the leg in the harness, and he used that leg to support himself while his other hand felt for the harness and found it. When two arms and one leg were in the harness, Aponi let go of the other leg and he slid into safety. He quickly pulled on the fishing line to straighten out the kite.

When he stopped shuddering he said, "I've got to remember that trick, with the mind and body. It's very helpful."

He pulled on the harness lines to test them and make sure both of them were tied in safely. He couldn't help smiling at Aponi. "Okay, let's go now."

They were up on the air, and Jimmy tried to get his bearings. He had never had a bird's-view of the area where he lived, so nothing looked familiar. Then he saw something that gave him their exact location.

"Over there. That's my house. Pull the left side down a little, we have to turn."

They pulled on the line from the left side of the kite, making that side turn down just enough for the kite to go in that direction.

"This is great. We can see everything. Look over there, that's Jo's house. That's the road into town, and that's the cliff Tommy fell from, way over there. After we land we have to head that way, and then follow the stream farther up to my tent. We won't be able to land by the tent; there isn't enough of a clearing over there."

Aponi stared out into the valley below and the rolling hills around them, and her eyes widened at what stretched out before her. "Now I know what it is like to be a bird, what a wonderful thing it is to fly. Do you like flying, Jimmy?"

"Sure I do, but I would rather be in a helicopter with a real pilot instead of me."

"What is a helly copter?"

"It's a flying machine. We have all kinds of machines like that in my world. I have a remote control helicopter at home. I'll show you later."

Jimmy continued to maneuver strings to get the kite going where they needed it to be. When they were over the stream, he said, "Okay, moment of truth. Now we're going to have to bring it down. Help me pull in the front line slowly, very slowly. We don't want to dive down too fast."

They tugged gently on the front line, bringing the tip of the kite down slightly. It was just enough to allow them to descend slowly. The sun was low in the sky as they came down to tree level.

"All those birds are flying like us. Your world is so beautiful, Jimmy. I wish never to leave here."

"Okay, Aponi. Now we have to pull in the opposite direction." He pointed her toward the back and both reached out to pull the line. The front of the kite tipped up, and it slowed down right above the trees on the bank of the stream.

"Now, Aponi, there's going to be a clearing ahead. As soon as we clear the trees, we're going to head for the middle and pull the front line again. This time we pull hard."

The kite approached the end of the tree line.

"There it is, Aponi. Now wait until we clear the trees and then pull. Okay, on the count of three. One, two, three, pull!"

Aponi and Jimmy pulled as hard as they could on the front line. The front of the kite dipped and it dropped very fast toward the ground.

"Aponi, quick! Pull the other way."

She froze as if not understanding the direction. The kite sped toward the ground. Jimmy wrested the line from her hands and jerked, bringing the back down. This leveled it off in time not to crash into the ground, but not in time to clear the bushes beyond the stream.

Crash! They flew right into a young raspberry bush. The impact threw Aponi over and out of the harness. She tumbled down to the next branch, and her weight caused that branch to give way and the next branch and the next branch until she rolled on the ground, stopping face down in the dirt. Jimmy disentangled himself from the harness and hopped down the branches.

He ran to Aponi, terrified that something might have happened to her, and knelt down. He slowly turned her over by the shoulders. "Aponi, are you all right?"

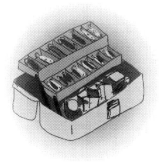

CHAPTER 8

AN EVENING ADVENTURE

At the foot of the raspberry bush holding the crashed kite, Jimmy stroked Aponi's forehead. "Please, please be all right," he muttered.

She opened her eyes and burst out laughing. "That was so much fun. Can we do that again?"

"I guess you're all right."

She sat up and threw her arms around his shoulders. "I am wonderful!"

"Well, I better go back up there and get the gear bag off of the kite. What?" Jimmy said, looking around. "Oh, no! We're on the wrong side of the stream. There's the cliff, and there's my rod, tackle box and Tommy's vest. See it over there, hanging on that branch, with a trail bar in the pocket." He rubbed his belly.

"First we eat, okay?"

"Then we have to cross the stream and find the Red Ring flowers, and I have no idea how we're going to do that."

Jimmy had forgotten all about the fallen tree that he and Tommy planned to climb over. It would have led them right back to the flower patch. All he could think of was that trail bar in Tommy's vest pocket.

Jimmy told her to sit and relax while he got dinner. He climbed up the cliff past their fishing gear and up the tree into the vest, and then he cut off a big chunk of the trail bar and covered it in a torn piece of the wrapper. He climbed back down with a feast for two. Jimmy unwrapped the chunk of trail bar and broke off a piece, then handed it to Aponi.

"This is very good, Jimmy. What is it?"

He finished the huge chunk he had in his mouth then said, "Everything that's good for you, plus a whole lot more. Just kidding, that's what the wrapper says. Anyway, it's going to be dark in about an hour or so; we have to move quickly."

Jimmy got the gear bag from the kite, and they climbed down the side of the cliff and went over to where the pool started at its most shallow part. Standing at the edge of the water with the last of the fishing line tied to a hook, Jimmy walked over to the water's edge.

"I know," he said. "I'll throw the hook as far over as I can and try to snag it onto a rock. We can pull ourselves across, at least to the end of the line. Hopefully, we'll be close enough to swim the rest of the way before we hit the stronger current."

Aponi was quiet for a minute, and then she said, "I have an idea."

"What? You don't like my idea?"

"Your idea would be fine, but we will get wet with your idea and might end up very cold."

"Okay, let's hear your idea," he said grudgingly.

"It's very simple. We go up to the top of the cliff where you just were. Then we shoot an arrow across the river, with rope and one of the hooks tied to it. We aim it over a low branch, hook it on, tie this side up, and then we can slide down and across."

"That's a good idea, except for two things. This hook is too heavy, and this is all the rope we have." He swung his arm up in a gesture to show the length of the rope. His eye followed his arm and he found himself gazing at his tackle box on the cliff up ahead.

"Wait a minute, there's my tackle box. I have a ton of string in there. I even have some really small hooks that won't be too heavy. You're a genius, Aponi, a genius."

She looked proud. They climbed to the top of the cliff and over the side of the tackle box. Jimmy took the smallest hook he could find and unrolled all the line they would possibly need. Aponi tied it to the arrow. They stood at the edge of the cliff.

"I took archery in school and was pretty good at it. What about you, Aponi? Can you shoot an arrow straight?"

"Not really, I just had good luck when I scared the raccoons away."

Jimmy tied the loose end of the line to the reel on his giant fishing pole. He cautioned Aponi to step back, and she did. He took aim and shot the arrow into the air. It went over the stream and into the ground just past a big log. He pulled on the line until the hook snagged the log.

"This is perfect, about a twenty-degree slant. Okay, all we have to do is tighten this line and slide to the other side." He refastened the line on the giant reel until it was taut.

But Aponi wasn't moving.

"All right, Aponi? Are we going or what?"

She moved her head to look at him, then back at the line, then back at him. "I don't know. It sounded easier when I had the idea. Now, how are we going to slide down the line without hurting our hands?"

"Got it covered. You see this strap on the pouch that we've been carrying all our stuff in? We just throw it over this line that leads to the other side, retie it onto the pouch, sit on the pouch and hold on. Our hands won't even touch the line. But we need to tie a second line to the reel, so that we can lower ourselves slowly and carefully. If we go too fast, we'll end up killing ourselves by crashing into the log."

Jimmy set to unfastening the strap, and he threw it over the fishing line and then tied it back to the pouch. He told Aponi to hold it in place while he got the second line ready.

He cut another piece of line, about the length of the one attached to the hook on the other side of the stream, and fastened one end to the pole's reel. Then he wound up the remainder on a makeshift reel using a broken piece of fishing lure he found in the tackle box.

"Okay, Aponi, you get on first," he said, laying the reel over the top of the pouch.

He held the strap at both ends, pulling it lower so Aponi could climb on. Once she was snugly positioned, he put his legs over the strap, one at a time. He jumped up and down a couple of times to make sure it held their weight.

"Are you ready, Aponi?"

She nodded.

"I'm going to wrap my arm around the leather strap, so my hands are free to let the line out and lower us down very slowly. All you have to do is hold on with both hands. Can you do that?"

She said nothing.

"Aponi, are you scared?"

"Is this where your friend fell and got hurt?"

"Yes, but that was different. He was hit with this big fishing rod that knocked the wind out of him. When he hit the water, he was probably already unconscious. I jumped in after him, and nothing happened to me."

"If I fall in, will you jump in and save me?" she asked, looking into his eyes.

"There's no way that I'm ever gonna let you fall in."

"I know, I will put my arm around you and hang onto the strap."

"Okay." He readjusted his position, so Aponi could hang on to his back. "Now all you have to do is hold onto me and the strap."

"I feel much safer this way. Thank you, Jimmy."

"Here we go," he grumbled.

It was twilight when they kicked off the cliff and started their ride down. Jimmy slowly turned the reel over and over to let the release line out. The little pouch moved down the line over the stream.

About one quarter of the way, Aponi became restless. "What is that?" she cried out pointing to a dark mass in the stream below.

"That, I think, is a trout. A very big brown trout, like the one we saw under the bridge. Don't worry, he can't jump this high, even if he can see us and thinks we're a dragon fly or something." Jimmy went back to unwinding the fishing line.

When they were a little more than halfway down the line, they were much closer to the water. "Look Jimmy, the fish is still under us."

He looked down at the trout and then at their potential landing site, and he started to let the line out a bit quicker. "He can jump this high, so let's not stick around here. Keep your eye on him while I bring us in. Let me know if that fish does anything funny."

"What do you mean anything funny?"

"Like jump."

At that instant she yelled at the top of her lungs, "Here he comes! Here he comes!"

Jimmy let go of the reel, and put both arms around Aponi. The reel flew up into the air and unwound. The pouch picked up speed and slid down the line just in time to escape being snatched by the trout. It jumped at them, missed, and bit the line they were sliding down. The weight of the big trout snapped the line as the fish fell back down. The sudden break left Jimmy and Aponi crashing down just short of land.

They splashed into shallow water unhurt. Although shaking,

Jimmy had the presence of mind to get Aponi scrambling toward the shore; he thought the trout was hot on their trail. As if, as long as they were touching the least bit of water, the fish could get them.

Once ashore, he surveyed for damage. "Are you all right, Aponi? Are you hurt?"

"I am all right. What about you?"

Jimmy gave himself a quick inspection before answering. "I'm fine except for being cold, and standing here in the dark, and being four inches tall, and—I mean, I'm good. No, I'm great, and that's all my brain has to say to my body. Right?"

"Right, Jimmy, but now I am cold, and it is starting to get dark. Maybe we should start moving. Which way?"

He poked with a dogwood twig in the stream until he hooked the pouch and pulled it from the water. "There is a flat path that we can take on this side; it's going to be much easier."

The moon started to come out from behind the clouds. In its light, Aponi ignored the frigid temperature and stopped to gaze at wonders rarely seen by the people of her village.

"That is so beautiful, Jimmy. The people in your world are lucky to have all of these beautiful moments in their lives."

"Don't you ever see the moon at all from your village, with the mirrors, I mean?"

"Sometimes when the moon is very bright, like now, we see it for a few moments. We see it the same way we see the sun, in the middle of our sky in one position."

She put her head down and continued walking in silence. Jimmy guessed that she was thinking about the village and her father.

"I'm sorry, I wish there was something I could do to make you feel better. I never realized that the sun and the moon could mean so much to someone. I guess we just take it for granted, but I won't any more. Do you realize that for the rest of my life, whenever I look at the moon, I'll be thinking about you and this very moment? Whenever I look at the sunrise again, I'll think about you and how your face was shining as you looked at the sunrise from the slate mountain this morning."

He could see her smiling in the moonlight.

"Thank you for saying those words, Jimmy. They were very nice. I will never forget about you, either."

He turned away from her with a strange kind of embarrassment. "Come on, we're almost there."

"Almost where?"

He ran ahead and found what he was looking for. "Almost here. Right here. Found it!"

"What, these flowers?"

"Like my mother says to me all the time, Aponi, it's time you grew up! You get it. This is the bulb of the Red Ring flower that we threw on the ground yesterday, you know, Magic Red Ring. The quicker we eat this, the quicker we can get bigger and find Jo. Here, I'll cut a piece for you."

Aponi looked at it for a while before taking a bite. They chewed and swallowed like they were taking medicine, both with looks of revulsion.

"This is awful, Jimmy. You should have given a warning."

He was inwardly pleased with his harmless prank. "If I told you it was terrible, would you have eaten it?"

"Maybe not," Aponi answered.

"That's why I didn't tell you. Come on, we should get going. We don't have too much farther to go." They walked for quite some time toward his and Tommy's campsite, where he knew there was a tent.

"When are we going to get bigger? How long does it take?"

"I really don't know. Yesterday, after Tommy and I ate it, we fell asleep for a couple of hours. It could take ten minutes, it could take two hours."

"I see the tent. Come on."

They ran the rest of the way in the moonlight.

"Is this your home?" she asked, looking up at this giant bubble.

"No. This is my pup tent. See the house up there, that's home," he said as he pointed far off past the trees, to the huge farm house that was all lit up, on top of a hill.

"Does your whole village live there? It's huge. You have all this land for farming, and for the children to play on?"

"No, just me, my parents and my little brother Jack. This is our farm. There is plenty of room for everyone in this world, it isn't as compact as your village. This land has been in my family for a long time. We own it, but somebody else works the land. My father works in the city, he's a lawyer, some kind of business legal adviser."

Jimmy stretched and let out a big yawn. "We should get some sleep. This has been a very long day, and the quicker we get into a sleeping bag the quicker we can start to warm up."

They made their way inside the tent, crawling through the flap that the two boys didn't close all the way yesterday when they left to go fishing. Once in the tent, they couldn't see a thing.

"Jimmy, I am afraid. Can you make fire with your hands again?"

"Oh yeah. The lighter is in my pocket." He clicked it, but it wouldn't light. "Oh darn, it's still a little wet. Looks like we're in the dark."

He threw the lighter on the ground and moved toward the sound of Aponi's voice. "Don't worry, there is nothing in here that we could get hurt on. The only things in here are some clothes and two sleeping bags. See?" He began to run around, jumping and rolling on the floor.

"Hey, this is fun, it's like a big moon walk bubble at the fair." Bang! He hit something really hard with his head.

"What was that noise? Are you all right?"

"Yeah, I'm okay. I guess there is something hard in here after all, and I found it," he said as he rubbed his head.

"When are we going to get big? I am very tired. I may not be awake much longer."

"Don't worry, I'm sure you don't have to be awake to get big.

Tommy and I weren't awake when we shrank. Besides, I'm getting tired myself. We could both use some sleep; it's been a long day. At least we have plenty of stuff to keep us warm, and we're totally safe in here."

Jimmy led her over to one of the giant sleeping bags and helped her to climb in and cover up, then walked to the other sleeping bag.

"Where are you going?"

"To the other sleeping bag. You know, we're going to grow soon. If we are too close, we'll be in each other's way, so I had better sleep over here. Good night, Aponi," he said as he covered himself up with the flap from the sleeping bag.

"Good night, Jimmy."

The next morning as the sun was rising, Jimmy opened his eyes and jumped up out of the sleeping bag.

"Aponi, are you there?" He gave the sleeping bag a nudge. *I knew she was too good to be true; it was just a dream.*

CHAPTER 9

THE GIANT WORLD

The tent flap opened, and a hand holding a plate of fresh-picked blueberries reached in. Jimmy gasped when he saw Aponi.

"Good morning, Jimmy. I would have waited for you to wake up, but I had to see what the world looks like from up here. It is very strange, but I have to say it is wonderful, just wonderful!" she shouted.

Jimmy was overcome with excitement himself seeing Aponi and knowing it wasn't a dream.

"Good morning," he replied as he took the plate.

"Jimmy, everything looks so different, it is all so small. These berries, I have never seen berries this small, they look like beads. They do not taste the same either. They are not as sweet when you eat the skin as well as the inside of the berry." She came into the tent and put the flap back down.

"It is chilly out there, but it is more beautiful than I could have imagined. I walked to the great river and saw a raccoon. It did not frighten me the least bit. There were all kinds of birds, a rabbit, even a fox. They are all so much more beautiful than they are in the books. This world is so different in every way except the weather. The mornings are cooler this time of year whatever size you are. We better build a fire. When we warm up a bit, we can find your friend Jo."

Jimmy grabbed at his pocket. "My lighter, I took it out last night and tried to light it. Then I threw it on the floor, it's probably around here someplace. Oh no, it's probably only about the size of a seed. Looks like we're going to have to warm up with the sun."

"I will build the fire. You just get some wood to burn."

"Can you really build a fire with a couple of sticks? I thought that you were kidding when you said you would show me how."

Aponi quickly swallowed the last few berries and undid the tent flap. "Come on," she said. "I will show you. It is not hard, you just have to be patient."

"That's just it, I'm not patient enough to get a fire started. I did it for my scout badge, but that was the last time."

Jimmy followed her to the spot he and Tommy had set up for a campfire two days ago, she laid a split log down and covered it with some dry grass.

Aponi got down on her knees and picked up a stick, put it between both her hands and held it down in the center of the log where she had put the grass. "There are two ways to make fire like this. One works faster than the other, but for the faster way we need some strong string."

Jimmy slipped back into the tent and came out with the spool of twine used for tying the tent to the stakes.

"You know, I always liked faster better when it comes to warming up," he said as he cut a length of twine at Aponi's direction.

He put the knife by the firewood. "Lucky for us I kept the knife tied to my belt, or it would be somewhere beside the lighter."

Aponi deftly tied the twine to one end of a stick, bent the stick a bit and tied the twine to the other end. She took the bow she had just made and put another stick along the twine, turned the stick, wrapping the twine from the bow once around it. She kept the stick from unwinding by holding it all in one hand while she picked up a flat rock with the other hand.

"Now you put the point of this stick into that dry grass on the log and hold it tightly in place by putting the flat stone on the other point. You then move the bow in the other hand back and forth, and that makes the fire stick turn very fast."

She moved the bow back and forth rapidly. "You must do it fast enough and long enough to heat up the point. When the point gets very hot, it will make a piece of the stick red hot and catch the dry grass on fire." As she said that, a light wind blew and a piece of grass burst into flames.

"You did it, I can't believe it. When we were at Scout training they only showed us the slow way, without the bow to turn the fire stick quicker. We just rubbed our hands together holding a stick in the middle, with the point touching the log and dry grass. I don't think anybody ever got it this quick."

Aponi laughed. "We show the little children in our village that way, it stops them from lighting too many fires. They don't have the patience to keep at it, so the stick never gets hot enough."

Jimmy felt a little resentment at her implying that he was a child, and his jaw tightened.

She noticed and quickly said, "When the children get older, we show them the faster way. I see that when you became a man, they showed you a fast way, too. They taught you how to make fire in your hand."

She means the lighter! Jimmy thought, and with his manly smile back in place, got firewood from the pile that he and Tommy had collected their first night there. He put a couple of pieces on the fire and sat next to Aponi.

"Now we will be warm in no time."

As he warmed up, Jimmy checked for injury by putting a hand on his forehead where he fell the night before. The bump from the fall had grown with him. Whatever he hit was unexpected. It wasn't something he and Tommy left there. Then he connected the dots.

He licked his lips. "Are you still hungry, Aponi? My mother must have dropped some munchies off inside the tent yesterday. That's what I hit my head on last night."

Without waiting for an answer, he went into the tent and came back out with a brown paper grocery bag. He sat back down and shuffled through the sack. "We have more trail bars, some fruit and fruit drinks and more healthy food. Ah, she also left some chips and soda, the good stuff."

Aponi looked at him like he was speaking another language. "I only know fruit. What is soda and chips and more trail bars?"

The corners of his mouth turned up in embarrassment at his thoughtlessness in once again forgetting how new everything in this world was to her.

"The trail bar is what we ate before we crossed the stream, and soda is something to drink. Chips? Well, I can't just tell you what chips are, you have to experience them for yourself. You'll love them," he said as he pulled out a bag of chips and ripped it open. "Here, try this."

She took the bag from his extended hand, reached in and pulled out a few chips. After biting into one, she made a face, chewed and swallowed and put the rest back into the bag.

"I would rather have some fruit, I know I like that."

She's the first person I ever met who didn't like chips. "I can't believe you don't like chips, especially these, they're sour cream and onion."

"I guess because they are sour, like you said."

Better to save the explanation for another time. He went into the food bag again, pulled out a banana and handed it to Aponi.

"What is this? This is not fruit."

He took the banana from her, peeled it and handed it to her again. "It is fruit, just not from around here. Try it. I promise you'll like it."

Aponi took a really small bite. "Mmmm, you are right, this is very good."

She took one bite after another until it was all gone. Then held her stomach and smiled. "That was a very good kind of fruit. What do you call it?"

"It's a banana. They grow down south, way down south."

"I am curious about this wonderful fruit. Where is the next town down south? Can we go there and get some bananas to bring back to the village? My mother and father would love them."

Jimmy finished the wad of chips he had in his hand, knowing it was going to take a while to explain this one.

"You see, Aponi, my world is bigger than you know. When I said ' way down south,' I didn't mean another town just south of us. I meant a few states away, or a different country. Like maybe a plane ride away, or at least a very, very long car ride."

"What is a plane ride and car ride? Can we go on this ride? Is it like your kite?"

Jimmy sat back against the log behind him and scratched his head. *Oh, brother. This is really going to take some time.*

Just as he was about to explain, he heard his mother calling him from the woods behind the tent. "It's my mom. Quick, get in the tent and don't make a sound."

With Aponi in the tent, Jimmy was zipping it up when his mother came into the clearing.

"Jimmy, why didn't you answer me when I called? And how come you didn't check in with me yesterday? You know when you camp out here you have to check in at least once a day. I came down looking for you yesterday. Your fishing gear was gone so I just dropped off the bag of goodies. Did you get it?"

Jimmy rubbed the bump on his head. "Yeah, I got it, right in the head," he said in a low voice.

"What was that you said?"

"I said that I got it, Mom. Thank you."

His mother moved to the front of the tent. "You'd better not be having chips and soda for breakfast. I packed you fresh fruit and juice."

"Yeah, I know. The bananas were a big hit."

"Where is Tommy?" she asked as she bent down to open the tent flap.

"Wait! You can't go in there!" Jimmy shouted.

"I can go wherever I want, mister. I'm your mother."

"Yeah, but you're not Tommy's mother, so I don't think you should see him in his underwear. Besides, he's sleeping."

She let the flap drop with a grin on her face. "Well, I wouldn't want to embarrass him. Oh, I forgot, I want you to come back to the house with me and say goodbye to your father. He's leaving this morning, and you won't see him for two weeks. He has to go to the city for all kinds of meetings." She started to walk back the way she came.

"Okay, Mom, I'll be right up. I just have to tell Tommy that I'm going to be gone for a little while, and I have to get some fresh socks on."

Jimmy's mother turned back with a stern look on her face. "You better be up there in five minutes, mister."

"I will, I promise."

Jimmy dove inside the tent. Aponi was sitting cross-legged on the sleeping bag. He waited for a minute or two, just to make sure his mother was out of listening range.

"Now Aponi, I have to go up and say goodbye to my father. Don't go anywhere, I'll be right back."

She looked panic-stricken. "Please hurry. I am going to be scared without you."

Jimmy sat next to her on the sleeping bag. "There is nothing at all to be afraid of. You are a giant now. You are in charge, not the animals. Remember the raccoon this morning?"

"You are right Jimmy, I am a giant now. I guess I will be just fine."

Jimmy zipped the tent flap behind him and headed to his house. He had a long walk, and the whole time he thought about the past two days. How Tommy was hurt, needing Jo-Pac's help and Aponi, the brightest spot of the whole camping trip. Jimmy started wondering how it would all work out and if he would ever see her again after they returned to the village for Tommy.

Jimmy's father was waiting for him at the back door. "Why the long face, Jimmy? Aren't the fish biting?"

"We did all right so far, I'm just a little tired. We went on a long hike yesterday."

His father came down the steps, sat on the bottom one and pointed at the step for Jimmy to sit. "Why don't you tell me about it? Where did you go?"

"We just went on a—well, I guess you would call it an adventure."

His father smiled. "An adventure, huh? What kind of adventure was it this time? Were you guys playing that lost-in-the-mountains game again, or was it cowboys and Indians?"

"You know I don't play cowboys and Indians any more, Dad. I'm thirteen years old. I'm too old for kid games. Besides, that would be rude. Jo is an Indian, and he is a good friend. A lot of Indians are very nice, and it's just plain wrong."

Jimmy's father stood up and threw his hands in the air. "All right. All right. I didn't mean anything by that. It's just a game you kids used to sometimes play. Jo is a very good friend of mine, too. You forget that we go way back. I testified at his trial along with Betty Ann's father."

Jimmy stood up. "I know, Dad, I'm sorry. I'm really tired. Anyway, I just came up to say good-bye and have a good trip. I gotta go, there are some more trout in the stream that have my name on them."

Jimmy kissed his father on the cheek and yelled to his mother, "Bye, Mom. I'll bring some trout home tomorrow if we don't eat them all." Jimmy turned and ran down the driveway, across the field and into the woods.

Just as he disappeared, his mother came out the door. "Where is that son of yours, Mike? I wanted to say good-bye."

"You know Jimmy. When it's time to fish, it's time to fish," his father said as he led his wife back into the house.

Jimmy jogged down the path, all the way to the tent.

"Hey, Aponi, time to go," he called as he opened the flap to the tent.

"Where did she go?" he said into an empty tent. "Oh no, I better find her, and quick."

CHAPTER 10

APONI MEETS BETTY ANN

Alone in the tent a little while before Jimmy returned, Aponi was worried. What will happen after his friend is better and they come back here? And what of this whole giant world she had discovered? It was a part of her now, and she liked it very much. She did not look forward to going back to the small world while Jimmy went to live with the giants.

It must not end, Aponi thought to herself. *Jimmy and I can stay friends forever. I will prove to my father that we belong in this world too, and we will all eat the Magic Red Ring and start out in this new world together.*

Aponi set out to bring her father some proof that this wonderful place was where the Takoda tribe belonged. She didn't know what she was looking for but knew she would recognize it when she found it.

She moved away from the stream where a path would likely be, and her instincts took her directly to the road. It looked like a path to somewhere, made firm by the feet of many horses. She reasoned that this path paralleled the stream, so to go right would be heading downstream. She knew what was downstream, Jimmy said the Delaware River, this would be the direction most likely leading to population.

This world is so very big, even for a giant like me, she thought. *I hope Jimmy does not worry, he will understand that I did this for the best. This is the only way to show my father we belong here, and the only way to stay with Jimmy.*

A thunderous noise filled the air. It was unlike any sound she ever heard. She hurried off the road and hid behind a tree, peering out at a sputtering pickup truck.

How does this cart move? There are no horses, no oxen, nothing is pulling it. And what is all that noise? How can those men stand to be in that thing, as loud as it is, although it does move very fast, faster than any of our horses.

She watched the monstrous noisy cart pass her and continue up the road. *Two men are riding in it. That must be the plane ride or the car ride.* She was proud of herself for figuring it out.

She came out of her hiding place and walked on in the same direction as the pickup. After crossing a small bridge over a stream that ran along the road, she found herself gazing at a strange house.

Though she had never seen one like it, this house was pleasing to look at and she knew it was beautiful. But it was not the proof she sought. Over the unpainted wood fence, she could see the tops of a few fruit trees in the back. She didn't know what kind of fruits they were, but she was sure they weren't bananas.

A thin girl who looked the same age as her was in the driveway. Aponi observed the girl from the road. She had curly blonde hair, long but not as long as Aponi's dark straight hair. She was dressed in pants made of the same denim fabric that Jimmy wore but much shorter and a white shirt with puffy sleeves, and white sneakers, as Jimmy called them, but no socks. The girl held a piece of rope in both hands and was throwing the loop it made into the air and jumping over the rope each time it came back to the ground. Aponi watched until curiosity got the better of her.

This will be all right, she thought, *everything in this world is wonderful.*

She walked up to the girl and introduced herself. "Hello, I am Aponi."

The girl stopped skipping rope and stared at Aponi walking up the driveway in leather pants with the bottom of her tunic torn. Her startled expression melted into a smile of graciousness.

"Hi. My name is Betty Ann Phlegmats."

Aponi took a step back thinking, *Phlegmats' domain? Is there going to be another one of those mean dogs around here somewhere? Maybe even a mean old man? Why did I think everything in this world is wonderful?*

She concluded that she had walked too far to still be in that horrible place, and Betty Ann didn't look mean. "Do you live here?" she asked.

"I live here with my folks. Where do you live?"

Aponi thought before answering, "I live in a small village, not too far from here." She was pleased with her cunning.

"What small village? What's the name of the village?"

"Helaku," she blurted out, "which means 'sunny day.'" It was the only thing that came to her head; besides, it was a sunny day.

"You're an American Indian, aren't you?" Betty Ann asked, squinting at Aponi's face.

"Yes, I am a Takoda Indian," Aponi answered proudly.

"I never heard of Takoda Indians before."

Aponi laughed. "We are a very small tribe."

Betty Ann extended her hand. "I am pleased to meet you, Aponi, the Takoda Indian from Helaku."

Aponi took her hand without hesitation and shook it as Betty Ann did. She decided to put her search for proof of wonderfulness on hold while she got to know another giant.

"So where do you go to school?" Betty Ann asked.

In a saddlebag? "Um, in my village parents teach their children."

"Oh, you're home-schooled. That's cool."

"Sometimes it is cool and sometimes warm."

Betty Ann chuckled. "That's funny. I like you, Aponi. Can you stay and visit for a while?"

"I would love to. Are you sure it will be all right?"

"Of course. Come on in the back. We have swings. Not that I ride on swings anymore, but sometimes it's still fun."

Aponi followed wondering what these swings might be. *If it is swinging over the river like Jimmy and I did yesterday, that was fun except for the fish biting at us.*

As they rounded the corner of the house and closed the gate, Betty Ann's mother called out from the back porch, "I'm going to let Satan and Lucifer out. Keep an eye on them."

Aponi froze with fear—those names sent a chill down her spine. She felt helpless and trapped. *Oh no, do I run? Do I stand still? What do I do?* She thought to herself, as she heard paws padding down the porch steps and into her direction. With her eyes shut tightly, she waited for whatever was going to happen.

Two dogs jumped up at her and knocked her down. They licked her face, tickling and making her giggle.

"They are puppies! Oh, look how beautiful they are, and very playful," Aponi said as fuzzy dogs with short ears and stumpy tails jumped all over her, each one trying to get more attention than the other. "How old are they?"

"About nine months. They were a Christmas present for my brother and me, and he got to name them because he's older. I wanted them to be Dusty and Rusty, but he named them after my uncle's dogs, Satan and Lucifer. I shouldn't have let him. Those dogs of my uncle's are just as mean as Uncle Horace is."

"I know."

"How would you know?" Betty Ann snapped.

"I meant I know dogs like that. There are two very mean dogs that live right outside my village."

"Oh. That must be creepy. Say, what time is it?"

"Time?" Aponi was puzzled but continued scratching the puppies behind their ears.

"Oh, you don't have a watch. I think it's about noon. Can you stay for lunch?"

"Thank you. I would like that very much. All I had for breakfast were blueberries and a banana."

"How healthy can you get?" Betty Ann stood up and started to walk toward the house. "I'll go check with my mother just to make sure it's all right."

Aponi went back to petting the puppies. A few minutes later Betty Ann came back with her mother.

She offered her hand. "Hello, I'm Betty Ann's mother."

"Hello, Betty Ann's mother, I am Aponi." Aponi took her hand and shook as Betty Ann had done earlier.

"Mrs. Phlegmats is fine. So, Betty Ann tells me that you are from a small town near here. Is that right?"

"Yes, I am from…" *What was it again?* "I am from Helaku. That means 'sunny day.'"

"Where exactly is He-la-ku? Far away?"

Aponi nervously stared at the ground. Obviously Betty Ann's mother was concerned about this girl all alone so far from home, just as Aponi's mother would be if a strange child appeared at their hut. "Not too far, just past Jimmy's house."

"Oh, you mean little Jimmy Farrell."

Aponi declared with uplifted face, "Yes, Jimmy Farrell." She hoped they were talking about the same Jimmy.

Betty Ann's mother studied Aponi with hands on hips. "You must be related to Jo-Pac. Are you his niece or something?"

Aponi recognized a name she could trust. "Yes, I am his niece."

Betty Ann's mother dropped her interrogatory manner and became cordial. "Then it's totally understandable that you ended up here, it's not too far. Well, I'm sure you and Betty Ann will have a nice time together. Come on in for lunch."

Inside the house, Aponi was amazed and looked everything over, once, twice and a third time. A million questions built up as they entered the kitchen but she didn't want to seem to out of place, so she held back.

The first thing she noticed was the polished stone slab running the length of the room at waist height where Betty Ann's mother stood putting spongy white squares on plates. The room was lighted when the wall was touched. Betty Ann's mother opened a large white box in which food was stored; a chill came out of the box.

Betty Ann turned the water on at the sink and washed her hands, and Aponi couldn't restrain herself any longer. "You have a spring in your house for washing?"

"What are you talking about?" Betty Ann asked. "It's a sink, don't you have one in your house?"

Aponi, mimicking Betty Anne, held the soap and made lather with the water running out of that metal tube. "All we have is a pitcher of water and a bowl."

Betty Ann rolled her eyes. Her mother whispered in her ear, "She is less fortunate, just look at her torn shirt. Don't make her uncomfortable."

"A pitcher, that's nice," Betty Ann chirped, reaching over to turn off the faucet after Aponi. "It's like camping all the time."

They sat down at the table, just as Betty Ann's mother was putting two plates of sandwiches down. "Do you like peanut butter and jelly?"

Aponi said, "Yes," hoping it was the right answer.

Betty Ann got up, and Aponi watched her open a wooden box above the stone slab and come back with a clear bag half full of yellow discs.

"How about some chips?" Betty Ann asked, rustling the cellophane package.

Aponi shook her head. "No, thank you. I already know what they taste like."

She followed Betty Ann's lead and put the PBJ sandwich to her mouth and took a bite. She scrunched up her nose. "Something is sticking to the top of my mouth." She put her finger into her mouth, scooped the peanut butter from the roof and licked it off her fingers. "It is very good. It tastes like fruit and something else."

Betty Ann giggled. "That something else is peanut butter, silly. That's what is sticking to the top of your mouth. And the stuff that tastes like fruit is fruit, it's strawberry jam. Didn't you ever have a peanut butter and jelly sandwich?"

Aponi shook her head. "No, but I am sure glad I am having one now. I also like bananas, and trail bars from your wor—" she stopped herself, "from your town."

"Yeah, trail bars are good," Betty Ann agreed.

After lunch, Aponi and Betty Ann were going out onto the porch when an orange and black monarch butterfly landed on the terra cotta flowerpot next to the steps.

"Is that a butterfly? It is the most beautiful creature I have ever seen," Aponi said, bursting with excitement. "My name means butterfly, and not until just now have I ever seen a live one."

"You've never seen a butterfly before?"

Aponi tried to sound as if she were correcting herself, as she squatted down by the flowerpot for a closer look. "I meant I've never seen one so beautiful. The ones in my village are plain, with very little color." She was thinking of the butterflies she had seen in the faded picture books in the saddlebag school.

"But isn't your village near—oh look, there it goes!"

Betty Ann's mother watched the two girls chase the butterfly as she was rinsing the lunch dishes and putting them into the dishwasher. As if struck by a sudden thought, she took the tea towel from its hook near the sink and dried her hands . Then she opened a drawer, and rummaged through it until she found her butterfly-shaped address book and looked up Jo-Pac's phone number.

The two girls in the yard were chasing monarchs and other butterflies, waving their hands in the air like mock butterfly nets. At the same time, the puppy Lucifer nudged a board in the fence that bordered the woods and disappeared through the opening it made. Satan, seeing he was alone, started whining and howling. This got the girls' attention.

Betty Ann ran to the fence and called out, "Lucifer. Lucifer. Where are you?"

"He went out where this board is loose," Aponi said, standing at the spot where Lucifer left the yard.

"We'd better find him before I get into trouble. My brother will be very angry with me if anything happens to his precious puppy. We can push the boards apart to make an opening that we can fit through." After following Betty Ann through the loose board, Aponi placed a stone in front of it to prevent Satan from getting out also.

Betty Ann peered into the dense woods and hesitantly walked toward the sound of Lucifer's barking. "Come on, Aponi, follow me."

CHAPTER 11

JIMMY GOES TO
JO-PAC FOR HELP

Meanwhile, Jimmy ran back to where the fishing rods were searching for Aponi. There were no other places to look, and he decided to walk along the stream toward the slate mountain.

"She's probably taking a banana to the village," he said as he moved out.

Some time passed, and Jimmy began to get panicky at the whole bizarre situation. His best friend was four inches tall and in a coma somewhere in a village nestled deep beneath a slate mountain. If that wasn't bad enough, he also had lost the daughter of the chief of that village.

All this just weeks before my fourteenth birthday. I guess thirteen is going to be a very memorable year for me. And Tommy said I would never achieve anything living in a small town. As usual, he found that making a joke about an impossible position was the only way he could keep a clear head.

He came to the bridge that marked the entrance to Phlegmats' domain. He thought to himself, *what else can I do? I don't know where else to look.* But entering Phlegmats' territory was such a horrible idea that he gave himself a few extra minutes to come up with another plan.

And it worked. *Wait, I got it. Jo will know where to look, plus he knows all about tracking and will help me find her. Besides, she wouldn't go anywhere near Phlegmats' domain. That much I'm certain of.*

Convinced that this was the right thing to do, he didn't step another foot toward that dreaded property line. Instead, he ran right to Jo-Pac's house, stopping for a second to grab one of the Red Ring flowers, bulb and all, to prove there was a red ring.

Jimmy thought he was in good shape, but he was bushed by the time he got there. He climbed up the steps to the porch of the modest wood-frame house and collapsed to his knees, dropping the flower beside him.

"Jo, Jo," he called out as more of a whisper.

The door opened. Jo-Pac bent down to help Jimmy to his feet. "Are you all right? What happened?"

"I'm all right. I'm just tired from running."

"Come inside for a drink."

"Jo, I've got to tell you something…"

Jo-Pac shushed him. "Here, sit on the sofa, relax and finish your water. Nothing's so important that it can't wait for you to catch your breath."

Jo-Pac's small house was sparsely furnished. The sofa, upholstered in muted brown and green stripes popular decades ago, was the major piece of furniture. To Jimmy at that moment it was the most luxurious sofa in the world.

He gulped in air, managed to down the water and collected himself. Jo-Pac looked at him suspiciously. Jimmy could almost read his mind. No doubt he expected to hear about a broken window or some other kind of mischief that always seemed to happen to these two boys.

"All right. What did you boys get into this time?"

Jimmy went outside and picked up the flower from the porch. He came in and sat back down on the sofa and reached for his knife, but it wasn't there. He remembered he left it at the camp on a log.

"Can I borrow your knife? I need to show you something very important before I fill you in on my problem."

"I thought that we had an understanding." Jo-Pac sat next to Jimmy and handed over his pocketknife. "I thought that you weren't going to kill any more of those beautiful flowers, especially over some old Indian folktale."

Jimmy cut the bulb through the center and put the knife in his pocket. "That was before I saw this. Check it out."

He separated the bulb into two halves, held one in each hand, and they both stared in silence at the bright red ring in the center until it was gone.

"Am I seeing right? Did that red ring disappear right in front of my eyes?"

Jimmy put the two halves back together and stuffed them into his jeans pocket. "Your eyesight is fine; you saw it disappear. I guess when the medicine man messed up, he was sort of on the right track."

Jo-Pac laughed and threw his hands toward Jimmy. "Come on. You don't expect me to believe that whole story, and you shouldn't believe it either. It is all a waste of time and beauty. Do you really think that if we eat this bulb, we will…?"

Jimmy interrupted. "Not only do I believe it, I did it. Tommy and I both did it."

Jo-Pac got a concerned look on his face. "What did you and Tommy do?"

"We ate one of the bulbs, and that's why I'm here. After we ate a bulb, we shrank down, and that is when the trouble started."

Jimmy filled him in on the whole story. About the time Jimmy was reaching the part where he and Yuma approached the slate mountain, the phone rang.

"Hold on, Jimmy. Let me get that."

Jo-Pac reached for the phone on the lamp table next to the sofa. "Hello…Oh, hi, Mrs. Phlegmats…What?…No, I don't…I am sure I don't know any girl named Aponi…Uh-huh."

Jimmy jumped up and covered the phone with his hand. "Please, Jo. Tell her Aponi is staying with you. She came with me from the village."

Jo-Pac pulled Jimmy's hand away. "Sorry, Mrs. Phlegmats, did you say Aponi?…Oh, I thought you said Melanie. Yes, Aponi is my niece… Okay. I will be over to pick her up shortly…Thank you."

He hung up the phone and went to the counter that separated the living room from the kitchen and pushed aside piles of unopened junk mail. "You may have won," the envelopes boasted.

"I don't believe it, Jimmy, not only did you go looking for trouble by eating one of those bulbs, you brought trouble back with you. What about Tommy? Where is he now?"

Jimmy put his head down. "That's why I came to get you. Tommy is in the Indian village. He's unconscious and has been that way since Friday afternoon. But they weren't going to let me leave. Aponi said she would help me if I took her with me. Her father said that I might be able to leave when I was older, but not now."

Jo-Pac stopped pushing around the envelopes and looked up at Jimmy. "You should have talked to the Chief; he would have helped you. Now where are those keys?"

Jimmy went to the counter and stood beside Jo-Pac. "Aponi's father is the Chief. He is the one that was going to keep me there."

Jo-Pac grabbed Jimmy by the shoulders and turned him so they were facing each other. "You mean to tell me that you took the Chief's daughter away from the village without permission and then let her wander off alone in this world?"

"No, I didn't mean to—I mean, I didn't let her wander."

"We have to go get her and take her back quickly. No telling what the Chief might do in this situation. She's at Betty Ann's. Let's go get her," Jo-Pac said as the key ring appeared from under a stack of receipts.

He put his brown suede hat over his long gray hair tied back in a ponytail, they ran out the door and hopped into the pickup truck. On the way, Jimmy picked up the story where he had left off. Jo-Pac listened to everything Jimmy had to say, and when he finished, the lecture came.

"Jimmy, how many times am I going to have to tell you that you shouldn't dive into situations without thinking them through? You have disturbed a peaceful tribe that was left alone for many, many years. I'm sure that if they wanted to come into this world, they would have found a way. Now they might be forced into this world, I just hope we can help them. And what about Tommy? It sounds like he's not doing so well. We're going to have to get some help for him too, which is going to be another tough situation. And his being so small doesn't help any."

Jimmy tried to defend his actions. "You don't understand. I wanted to wait till we talked to you, but Tommy called me chicken."

That was all he had to say. Jimmy knew that Jo-Pac understood the one thing Jimmy Farrell, like his father Mike Farrell before him, would not tolerate, was to be called a chicken.

"Well, Jimmy, you are going to have to learn that you have to be your own person, not the person other people want you to be. You're a smart young man, but sometimes your body doesn't do what your mind tells it to do."

Jimmy quickly turned his head in recognition of Aponi's theory. "Aponi says the body feels the way the mind tells it to feel. I guess that is pretty much the same thing. If my mind feels it is wrong to do something, I need to make sure my body doesn't do it. I should have just listened to my first instinct, but then I never would have met Aponi." Jimmy felt his face light up when he mentioned Aponi.

Jo-Pac looked over to his passenger at that moment. "You really like her, don't you?"

Jimmy shrugged it off, trying not to let on how he felt. "She's all right, cool to hang out with. She's not like the other girls around here, we have fun together."

"Sure, sure." Jo-Pac just smiled.

CHAPTER 12

DEEP WOODS
AND DEEP TROUBLE

ꓐack at the Phlegmats' house, Betty Ann and Aponi were just heading off into the woods following the sound of Lucifer's barks. Lucifer sounded farther away with every step they took. When he couldn't be heard anymore, Betty Ann took a look at the surroundings and folded her arms across her chest as if she got a chill. Her jaw dropped.

"We're lost. What are we going to do? I have never been this far in the woods before."

Aponi thought she heard the sound of rain in the distance. She held up her hand. "Quiet. Do you hear that? It is the river."

"What river? The only river we have is the Delaware, and that's a far way off. There are a couple of little streams around here, but that's all."

"Well then, it is a stream. We are not lost. It is coming from this direction."

Aponi went toward the sound pushing shrubbery out of the way. Betty Ann followed taking small steps until they reached a gently flowing stream.

"This is our way out," Aponi exclaimed. "All we have to do is follow the stream to Jimmy's house and walk back to yours. We just have to make sure we do not run into one of your uncle's dogs."

"You're the guide, lead on. But how do you know where my uncle's dogs are? Oh well, never mind, just get us out of here. Which way?"

"Upstream, against the current," Aponi confirmed.

What Aponi didn't remember was that she crossed a stream right before she reached Betty Ann's house. That was the stream that led to Jimmy's house, this stream led deep into the back woods and deep into trouble.

Aponi was totally unaware and decided to teach Betty Ann a game. "Do you play stone-hopping?"

"No, what's that?"

"You have to jump on rocks. One foot has to be off the ground at all times. If your feet touch soil, you lose."

"Like hopscotch. I can play that." Betty Ann hopped to another rock and held one foot behind her. "Can it always be the same foot?"

They were going far into the woods, where the trees' high branches overhead blocked out more and more of the sun, making it darker and even harder to pick out possible landmarks.

"Aponi, are you sure we are going the right way?"

"I think so. We will go a little farther. If we are still unsure, we will turn around."

"I don't want to play stone-hopping. I'm scared, and it isn't fun anymore."

Aponi, scared as she was, felt she had to be brave. She tried to take Betty Ann's mind off the situation, and thought for a while about some common interest to talk about. But they knew so little about each other that the only thing that came to mind was their common friend.

"So, Betty Ann, do you know Jimmy well?"

Betty Ann took a minute to answer. That was okay with Aponi, because it meant she was thinking about something else besides being lost.

"Yes. We have lived here forever, and so has Jimmy. My grandparents built the house we live in, and Jimmy's grandparents built the house they live in. But Jimmy's and my grandparents all moved down south after they retired. Mr. and Mrs. Farrell, Jimmy's parents, went to school with my parents, and I go to school with Jimmy."

Aponi grew interested in the history and interrupted Betty Ann. "What about my Uncle Jo? How long have you known him?"

"Well! Let me tell you," she said conspiratorially, as if about to get into gossip mode. "My parents have known him since they were about our age. He used to work for Jimmy's grandfather on his farm. One day, not too long after he started, he went fishing with Mr. Farrell and my father. When they got home, the police came and took him to jail for murder. Mr. Farrell and my father testified that he was with them all day and couldn't have done it, but it didn't make any difference. He got out about two or three years after I was born. Everybody thinks that Mr. Farrell and my father lied, but my dad would never lie."

Boom! Came the thunderous sound from the other side of the stream.

Aponi pointed up a hill. "That loud noise came from up there. That is not a natural sound. If we head that way we may find someone who can help."

"I wouldn't do it myself, but you're the guide. I'm following you."

Near the top of the hill, male voices could be heard from the other side. Aponi couldn't make out any of the words but didn't want to expose them to possible danger.

"Careful," she whispered. "We will see if it looks like we can trust them."

Really scared now, the girls got quiet but kept going. At the top, the hill got steeper. Betty Ann lost her footing. She fell and slid down toward the stream.

She only traveled a few yards, but it made lots of noise over the gravel. Aponi couldn't think about that; she was only concerned about Betty Ann. It looked like she took a rough fall.

Aponi ran down after her. "Are you all right? Can you stand up?"

She helped Betty Ann back to her feet and brushed off the dirt and leaves from her clothing.

"Aponi, do you think they heard us?"

A deep, raspy voice came from right behind them. "Yep, we heard ya, little girl."

Aponi whirled around. Standing in front of them was the second scariest man she had ever seen. This man was a big, mean-looking, old American Indian, with a scar that ran the length of his arm. And he had a rifle.

Then, the first scariest man Aponi had ever seen came over the top of the hill: Horace Phlegmats, and he was carrying a rifle too. Betty Ann didn't seem to be relieved to see her uncle.

I guess he scares her as much as he scares me, Aponi concluded, as she looked into Betty Ann's face.

"Why, if it ain't my little niece. I haven't seen you since Christmas dinner. How are those little puppies? Y'all call them Satan and Lucifer just like my babies, right?"

"Hello, Uncle Horace."

"Whatcha kids doin' out here anyway?" Horace roared. "You don't belong here."

Betty Ann stared at the ground. She answered with a whimper. "We're lost, Uncle Horace."

She must be afraid to look at him, Aponi thought.

"Speak up, child, I can't hear you," Horace said impatiently.

Aponi looked right into that scary old man's eyes and shouted, "She said we are lost!" After speaking, she realized she was just as scared as Betty Ann.

"Quite the big mouth, for a little Injun girl. Wouldn't you say so, Johnny?"

Johnny Blackfoot was his name, a cold and violent man, as mean as they came. He committed many crimes in the area but always managed to make it back to his hiding spot in the woods before getting caught.

"What'd I tell you? Don't use my name in front of people," Johnny growled at Horace.

"Don't worry, they's kids. They don't know you." He turned to the girls. "You kids get in the back of the truck. I'll take you home in a little while."

What is a truck? Aponi thought to herself as they went over the hill. She stopped when she saw it.

It is that monster I saw on the path. Well, it is not rumbling now, and it seems quite tame.

Betty Ann looked over the truck's panels. "Eew, that's gross," she burst out and held her stomach.

Aponi went to see what was there. It was a dead, antler-less adult white-tailed deer. She recognized it from pictures in one of her books back at the village. She wasn't squeamish about being around hunted animals; the braves in her village hunted as well, mostly small critters that a hunting party could manage to overcome. That was how her tribe ate and the source of much of their clothing, but killing for any other reason was an offense to her and the whole world.

"What happened? Did you kill it?" she asked with concern.

Horace bent over and looked right into her eyes from about two inches away. "He musta got hit by a car and made his way back to the woods, but he was suffrin' so we had to put him down. It was a kindness."

Johnny came round the side of the truck with the blanket used to cover the seats in the cab, and he and Horace pulled the deer to one side of the truck bed and covered it up with the blanket.

"There, now you don't have to look at it," grizzly-voiced Johnny Blackfoot said.

"Get in the truck," Horace ordered.

Aponi considered not obeying. Betty Ann was repulsed by the deer and having to sit near it. But she felt responsible for Betty Ann. They didn't know where they were, and these two men did. If there was any chance of getting back, it was with them.

There may be bears in these woods, Aponi thought to herself. She had heard horrifying tales about them back in the village. She knew two girls were no match for a hungry bear foraging in the woods. She was worried about Betty Ann, who was exhausted, frightened by the whole forest experience and seemed prone to slipping; an injury could put them both in danger. Horace, scary as he was, certainly wouldn't hurt his blood relative.

In a split second, Aponi decided she had enough of wandering aimlessly through the woods and just wanted to get the adventure over with. "Let us go with them," she told Betty Ann. "They know the way, and we do not."

"That's right," Johnny called over his shoulder while climbing into the passenger seat. "We know the way."

Aponi felt a strange uneasiness while stepping into the back of the truck and learned for the first time what it was like to have butterflies in her stomach. Horace fastened the tailgate in place. In the cab, Horace and Johnny hung their rifles on the rack attached to the back window.

Aponi touched the blanket covering the deer with the back of her hand. "Still warm. This was recently killed."

"That must be the crash we heard."

Horace opened the back window. "Now, you two younguns hold on," he yelled as they took off, even deeper into the woods.

Aponi knew she was having a car ride or a plane ride, and whichever it was, she did not like it. The metal beast made loud, unpleasant noises as if its stomach was rumbling, and what a large stomach it must be to supply enough energy to move four people on its own. This beast bounced around like the medicine man doing a rain dance. Its huge wheels were like the wheels on the cart that moved the door to the village.

Horace had left the back window open; as the truck slowed down, Aponi could hear them talking.

"Why'd ya bring'em here, Horace? They got no business here, what if they..."

"What if they what, Johnny? Ya think anybody is gonna listen to two dumb kids? If anybody gave younguns the time a day, they'd a listened to my kid brother and that Farrell punk. And they'd a still been looking for you, instead of sending that Jo-Pac away. He did an awful lot of time for ya, remember? And don't ya forget who pulled up in a nice fast car and saved your sorry hide back then. You can thank me again if you like."

The truck hit an especially rough spot, and the deer shifted. Johnny turned to check, and Aponi was still looking in at them. He yelled at her to sit back down and slammed the window shut. Aponi pondered what she heard. She knew the name Jo-Pac, but didn't understand what these men were saying about him.

The truck traveled way back in the forest on a dirt road and came to a stop near an old abandoned lumber mill. There was a cabin set back in the woods on the side of the mill, and a path on the side leading further back into the woods.

"You kids stay here. We're gonna take this poor deer and give him a proper burial. Come on, Johnny, take hold of a leg and help me drag it down by the barn.

"Now remember. You two kids stay here, and we'll get you home in no time," Horace yelled as the two men dragged the deer.

As soon as they were gone, Aponi asked, "Who is Johnny?"

"I don't know. A friend of Uncle Horace, I guess. I've never seen him before. If he smiled, he wouldn't look so scary. As a matter of fact, he would look a lot like Jo. Don't you see the resemblance?"

"No," Aponi answered. Then to avoid any questions about why she didn't know what her uncle looked like, she said the first thing that came to her mind, "Why is your uncle so mean?"

"Well! I guess he's always been like that, just a bad seed. My father said he's always been trouble. It scares me that I see some of him in my brother. And that we have to share the farm with him. When Grandma and Grandpa Phlegmats moved south, they gave the farm equally to both their sons. My father has a job in town, so Uncle Horace runs the farm. We live in the house Grandpa built, and Uncle Horace has a cabin down on the farm."

"Has he ever hurt you?"

"Oh, no. I don't think he would hurt his family."

"Then why are you afraid of him?"

"He's crazy, and he talks to himself. And he has told people that he's seen little tiny Indians on the farm, on little tiny horses. I told you he was crazy. Have you ever heard of such a thing?"

Aponi just stared back, unable to utter a word about little Indians. "I will go see what is keeping them."

Betty Ann grabbed her arm. "Didn't you hear what they said? They said to wait here, and that is exactly what we better do."

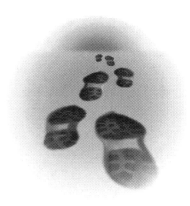

CHAPTER 13

THE SEARCH BEGINS

Jimmy and Jo-Pac arrived at Betty Ann's house, and knocked on the door. There was no answer, so they peeked over the fence into the yard. Betty Ann's mother was standing at the back fence watching the woods but turned her attention to the front when a car drove by. She came across the yard and opened the gate.

"They're gone. The girls are gone," she said as she turned and headed back in the direction from which she came.

"What's the matter, Mrs. Phlegmats? Where did the girls go?" Jo-Pac asked as he ran up to her.

"They were here a little while ago, right before I called you. They must have gone looking for the puppy Lucifer. He sometimes gets through the fence and goes for a walk, but he always comes back. I am more than a bit worried. Betty Ann never goes far into the woods; it frightens her."

Just then, Lucifer came walking out of the woods and back into the yard around the loose board like it was an everyday thing. Satan joined him and nipped at him to start a romp, but after his hike Lucifer was in no mood to play.

"Don't worry," Jo-Pac said, "we'll find them. They probably lost track of time and wandered too far into the woods."

Jo-Pac and Jimmy pushed the board aside and dashed into the woods. They walked straight in about fifty yards before Jo-Pac stopped and crouched down to look at the ground. "It's not going to be easy to find their trail with all the slate and rock that's around here."

With nothing to go on, they followed what appeared to be a trail of bent grass, looking on ahead as they walked in order to catch sight of the girls if they were still in the vicinity. The stream could be heard in the distance, but the trail seemed to be getting cold.

Jo-Pac bent down and inspected the ground again. He reached with a finger and pushed up the brim of the brown fedora to look at Jimmy.

"I don't know, Jimmy. Would she have gone to the stream?"

"I don't think so. She already crossed our stream back on the road, you know, the stream that runs through our property. So she would have known she was going out of the way. I bet she went another way."

"Well, don't forget they were chasing an animal, so they probably didn't have a destination in mind. I can't tell a thing from the dirt on the ground; there isn't any trail here at all. Either they were walking a different way, or they kept up off the dirt and grass, walking on top of all the stones."

Jimmy considered this possibility. It was quite plausible, as the whole area was littered with big sheets of slate, and one could easily go on for miles without ever touching the soil.

"Well, you know her better than I do," Jo-Pac declared. "Let's head away from the stream."

They turned around and went off toward Jimmy's house in the direction of Phlegmats' domain, but actually they were headed in the opposite direction of where the girls were. They made it all the way to Phlegmats' domain without seeing a trace of them. As they were approaching the old tractor bridge, Jimmy recognized a huge mountain of slate.

"That's it, look over there. That's where the village is, you know, the little Indian village. It's funny, I never noticed that big mountain of slate before. So let's go get Tommy." Jimmy took a step toward the mountain as he pulled the two halves of the Red Ring Flower bulb out of his pocket.

Jo-Pac put a hand on Jimmy's shoulder to stop him. "All in good time. Do you really want to go over there and maybe see the Chief? What will you say when he asks about his daughter? There is no telling what he will do when he finds out you lost her. You may be endangering Tommy. I think we better find the girls first."

"Oh, I didn't think of that." Jimmy turned and started walking toward the bridge, tucking the two halves back into his pocket. He sure didn't want to run into Chief Yuma, regardless of the fact that he was about twenty times bigger than the Chief. "Good idea, Jo. Maybe we should find Aponi first, and Betty Ann. At least the two demon dogs aren't out and about."

Jo-Pac nodded. "Yeah, Horace is probably out and left the dogs locked in the barn. But if they were out, you might move a little faster." Jo laughed and gave him a nudge to get him moving.

Jo-Pac kept his eyes on the ground for signs that the girls had been there. When they passed the bridge he said, "They didn't come this way. We better backtrack to behind Betty Ann's house. Either they went farther upstream or they are back at the house."

They turned back the way they came, past Jimmy's house and deep into the woods. Jo-Pac still kept looking for signs but found none. After a little while, they reached the original spot where they had turned away from the stream. It was close to Betty Ann's house, so Jimmy ran to the yard and came back reporting the girls were still gone.

"All right, Jimmy. Let's check over by the stream."

As they approached the stream, Jo-Pac said, "This has more promise. See those broken branches on the shrubs. They are broken up high. Could have been a deer, but could have been a person too."

He wrapped his thumb and forefinger around a twig and snapped it. "Compare this to the other broken branches. There is no difference, meaning the breaks are fresh. Someone or something has been through here very recently."

They walked to the stream and split up. Jimmy went in one direction, and Jo-Pac went in the other. Jimmy walked about ten feet when he spotted something.

"Look, Jo, over here," he said as he bent down to inspect the disturbed ground.

Jo-Pac ran over to where Jimmy was crouched. He bent down. "Show me what you found."

"They were here," Jimmy said, pointing to an imprint in the mud along the stream. Two clear prints were visible, one a sneaker and the other a flat sole.

"That's a moccasin print. I've seen enough of them in my lifetime to recognize it. They probably kept to the rocks, but it looks like they were definitely headed upstream."

They were at the place where the girls started playing the stone-hopping game, so there were no more footprints to find. Jimmy was getting frustrated by the lack of signs.

"I can't believe this. What happened to them? Did they just disappear?"

"I told you it would be hard to track in this rocky terrain. What we have to do is keep going until we hit on something else."

Finally they arrived at the spot where the girls heard the shot.

"They went up the hill," Jimmy said excitedly.

Jo-Pac verified that sneakers and moccasins had traveled there. "The imprints are not very deep although the ground here is somewhat soft. They were walking slowly and quietly, probably trying not to disturb something."

He pointed ahead to the spot where Betty Ann had slid down the embankment. "See those marks? Even though it's mostly gravel, you can tell something was sliding by the long impressions, as if someone lost their footing."

"And here where the gravel ends, there are footprints." Jimmy looked closer. "These are different."

"I don't like this!" Jo emphasized. "There are more over here: larger, hard-soled shoes. Looks like these footprints belong to a couple of men, and they were walking alongside the girls. They went this way."

Jimmy slapped a hand over his open mouth and removed it slowly to ask, "What does it mean?"

"They got into a vehicle over here. And a few yards that way there's some blood."

"They've been hurt!" Jimmy clenched his fists and waved them.

"Hold on, hold on. It's animal blood; see this hair on the ground?" He picked it up and rubbed it in between two fingers. "It was a deer, and it was dragged to the vehicle."

"What has happened to them?" Jimmy stammered. He unclenched his fists but felt weak, and his face lost its color.

Jo-Pac took him by the shoulders. "Look, Jimmy, you need to be strong, and you need to stay calm. Can you do that?"

"Uh-huh," Jimmy said, but he didn't know if he could. He felt like his knees were going to buckle, and he took a few steps back until he brushed against a young pine tree. He leaned against it to steady himself.

"The tire tracks go toward Old Mill Road, and I have a hunch about what is going on. I am going to follow these tracks. I want you to go back to Betty Ann's house and see if the girls are home. If they are, wait for me. If they are not there, I want you to call the police. Are you listening, Jimmy?"

"Yes, you want me to go to Betty Ann's and call the police."

"Tell them to send a car to take a look up Old Mill Road. Tell them that's where the missing girls might be. Get a hold of yourself, Jimmy. You have to do this."

"I'm okay." Jimmy stepped away from the tree just to prove to himself that he wouldn't fall over. "Are they in danger?"

"I don't know. But we have to act quickly."

"I want to go with you and find them."

"No, there may not be time. Jimmy, you have to be brave. You're not chicken, are you?"

CHAPTER 14

THE SECRET BARN

*A*poni's patience was wearing down. "They should have been back by now. It cannot take this long to bury a deer. I want to go and see what can be keeping them."

Betty Ann didn't say anything until Aponi hopped off the truck.

"Wait! Where are you going?"

"If you want to stay here, you can. I will just tell the men to hurry up." Aponi started to walk toward the cabin.

"I'll come with you. I don't want to stay here alone."

They followed the path Horace and Johnny had taken. At its end was the cabin; it was old and run down with boarded-up windows. As they approached the cabin, they could see an old barn at the end of the path alongside of it. There was nothing else back there but woods, and the sound of a large river that wasn't too far off.

Aponi and Betty Ann reached the cabin. Betty Ann tried the door; it was locked.

"Where could they be?" Aponi wondered.

"Well, you don't bury a deer in a cabin. Listen, do you hear that?"

They could hear a faint raspy noise over the sound of the river rapids; it was coming from the barn. Aponi led the way. She was afraid to try the door again and circled the barn looking for a place to peek in. She found that place at the back of the structure, where a low plank was missing.

She motioned Betty Ann to join her in spying. At the near side, on the dirt floor, they saw farm equipment, a rusted-out old time sports car and a generator humming loudly. Two chest-type freezers were plugged into the noisy generator.

At the front of the barn, the two men wearing butcher coats covered in blood were standing over a half-skinned deer on a wooden table. Johnny was skinning away. "I don't know why you just didn't leave them there, Horace. Now they know about me, and they know about the mill. Sometimes I think you're as stupid as everybody says."

Horace walked around the table and looked him in the face. "That there's my niece, I got a family responsibility. You being a savage don't understand a thing about responsibility, and I reckon ya never will. Remember, you dumb Injun, if it weren't for me, you'd be in jail right now. Ya think you would have gotten out after only twenty years. Ya don't even know what good behavior is."

"Don't give me that responsibility nonsense; I know how much you hate your brother and his family. And how many times do I have to hear you say if you didn't stop and pick me up, I'd a gone to jail?"

"I don't rightly know," Horace admitted. "Maybe till you're grateful."

Johnny Blackfoot wandered into town many years ago, a couple of months before Jo-Pac. He was a hardened criminal and ran wild, stealing and hurting people. Then he robbed a grocery store and shot a man, the one Jo-Pac got blamed for. He figured it was time to lay low, so he had been hiding in the woods ever since. He would go into other towns when he needed something, or have Horace pick it up. Horace was his buddy. Neither one had any other friends, and they were both lowlifes.

Horace was an accidental part of the robbery, all those years ago. He happened to drive by in the flashy sports car he had just stolen when Johnny ran out of the store. Johnny turned the corner and ran right into the car, smashing his arm into the window, breaking the glass and giving himself that long scar. Horace let him in the car and hid him from the law, for a percentage of the take. And that was how they hooked up. They were partners ever since in a number of ventures. At the present time their business was poaching, and business was good.

Horace stepped back. "All that don't matter none. If them girls turn up missing, they'll get a search party together and come a-looking, and whacha think will happen to us if the law comes and sees all the goodies we got here?"

"After we finish here, I'll take 'em home, and that'll be the end of that. Them younguns'll be so happy that they won't even remember ya. You gonna stay here whilst I bring 'em back. If they do say anythin' about ya, I'll say it was their overactive imagination, ya know, being scared of the woods and all." Horace chuckled as he bought a huge meat cleaver down, separating a leg from the rest of the body.

Betty Ann gasped and jumped back into a pyramid of split oak firewood. The logs tumbled from the woodpile and thumped into the barn wall one after the other.

Horace jumped back, and the cleaver in his hand barely missed Johnny's neck. Johnny went straight for the missing plank where a stream of light came in.

He bent down and peered through the opening. "There they go running back to the cabin. It's them two brats. I told you they was trouble. They saw it all, they heard it all. What are we going to do now?"

Horace grabbed him by the shoulder, pulled him up to his feet and started yelling in his face. "How 'bout if we go stop 'em for now? Sound good, ya dumb Injun?"

Johnny got right in Horace's face. "I told you, don't call me a dumb Injun, you crazy old man."

Horace opened his mouth and snapped it shut as if he were about to start yelling again but stopped himself. "Why don't ya shut up long enough for us to catch up with them girls?" he said in a voice well below a shout.

When they got to the cabin, the girls were sitting on wooden faded green Adirondack chairs on the porch. They stood up as the two men approached, as if they were there the whole time.

"Betty Ann and I were waiting here for you, we got tired of waiting in the truck." Aponi grinned, hoping they would buy her story. In truth, Aponi wasn't any more scared than before. They hadn't heard anything that was said in the barn over the noise of the generator.

"All right," Horace said as if everything was okay. "Come on in the cabin and I'll get ya somethin' to drink."

Johnny grabbed him and whipped him around. "What are we doing? Running a nursery?"

"They's probably thirsty. We ought to be good hosts, don't ya reckon so?" Horace winked at him.

Johnny winked back. "Oh, yeah. Sure, a nice cold drink. Let's all have one, except make mine a beer. We got any on ice?"

Horace unlocked the cabin door. The inside wasn't totally dark; a few holes in the boards over the windows let some sun filter in. Horace lit a lantern that was hanging by the door. It illuminated old wood furniture along the bare walls of the room. A door led into another room.

"Go in that room," Horace said. "The drinks are in there; help yourself."

Betty Ann, seeming pleased, did not question him but ran right into the room. Aponi did not believe Horace's change in personality and still had no trust in this scary man. She proceeded with caution, inching up to the door and peeking in.

By this time, Betty Ann was on her way back out. "There aren't any drinks in here, there's nothing but an old cot."

Horace shoved them back through the door and slammed it behind them. "Gotcha!" he yelled as he bolted the door. "And now all's I need to do is figger out what to do with ya little brats."

In the little room, Betty Ann backed up into the corner and started bawling. "What are we going to do now?"

Aponi patted her on the back. "First, tell me what this is about? Why do you think they locked us in here?"

"They are," Betty Ann sniffed to stop her nose from running. "They are poachers."

"What does that mean?"

"Oh, don't you know anything? It means they kill animals and sell the meat and skins. It's against the law. I heard of someone who spent five years in jail for doing that."

Aponi didn't understand what this had to do with them. She went back to the door to eavesdrop in the hopes of finding out what was behind it.

On the other side of the door, Horace sat with his elbows on the table, hands covering his face. "They must have heard more than they should have. I'm getting worried."

"We need a plan. This here business is too profitable to risk a couple of kids ratting on us and spoiling it all."

"What the heck we gonna do, Johnny? How are we gonna get out of this here mess?"

Johnny walked over to the table and slammed his fists down. "I think you already know. We only have one way out, and that's to get rid of them brats. You always wanted your brother Ronnie and his family dead anyway. Just think, after all this is over, we can work on getting rid of your brother's other little brat, then him and his wife. And then the farm will be yours, all yours."

"I don't know Johnny, it all sounds too easy. Ya reckon it could really work? I mean I ain't scared to get rid of them girls, it's getting caught that worries me."

In the other room, Aponi had her ear pressed against the door, listening. Betty Ann sat on the cot, sobbing.

"Are we ever going to get home, Aponi?" she asked, as she wiped tears with her fingers.

"We are going to leave this place right now," Aponi promised.

Betty Ann lifted the hem of her white shirt and dabbed a corner on her eyes and wiped her nose with a puffy sleeve.

Aponi felt around the old wall boards, looking for a loose one. One after the other, she checked the boards. At last a board moved as she pushed on it. She pushed a little harder, hoping not to make too much noise. The board came loose and fell outward into bushes that surrounded the house. She stiffened, waiting for the crash, but the board hardly made a sound.

"We need to get out of here right now," she whispered.

Betty Ann didn't move. "What if they locked us in here to keep us safe, until they can take us home?"

Aponi was forced to tell the truth. "I heard that man tell your uncle that they have to kill us. Then they are going to kill your whole family so Horace can have the farm. We have to go before they come for us!"

She pushed Betty Ann through the hole in the wall and then went through herself. They skedaddled into the woods, where Aponi looked for the thickest parts for cover.

Inside the cabin, Johnny appeared to be getting through to Horace on the idea of being a farm owner. "What do ya say, Horace? All we have to do is throw them off the cliff into the river with rocks tied to their feet. We'll get them where the water is so deep there that the bodies won't ever be found. Then we lay low for a while and take care of the rest of the family in a few months."

Horace stood up with a confident look on his face. "All right. It looks like ya got it all figgered out. I reckon it could really work, but we're gonna have to do it right."

He unlocked the door to the other room and kicked it open. "All right, you snot-nosed kids, let's...Where in the heck are they? They're gone!" Horace rubbed his unshaven chin.

Johnny stepped into the room and pointed at the back wall. "They went out that way. We gotta get 'em back right now!"

Horace tried to go out through the hole in the wall. He put a foot through and got stuck. He pulled at another plank, but the nails held fast. He was still fighting with it when Johnny jerked him back in and pushed him to the cabin's front door.

Behind the cabin, they immediately found the girls' trail. "This way, Horace, this way."

The girls had a good head start, but they were getting tired of running.

Betty Ann collapsed. "I don't think I can go on much farther."

Aponi stopped and took a deep breath, realizing she was tired herself. "We should go on just a little farther."

She was just guessing, but it seemed to give Betty Ann encouragement. At least they were able to keep walking a while longer.

Upon reaching a steep hillside, Aponi came up with an idea. "We are going to climb up to where the ground gets rocky and come back down walking backward. We will continue to walk backward until we get to those bushes, over there," she said, pointing to a patch behind them. "And with a bit of luck, your uncle and his friend will think that we kept going up the hill on those rocks."

"Well, I don't have a clue what you're talking about. But you seem to know what you're doing so far. So if you think it will work, I'm with you."

Aponi led the way trudging up the hillside about fifty feet, to a ledge. "Now, go back down, backwards, and put your feet in the same prints you made going up."

"I knew there was a catch. How am I supposed to do that?"

"Look behind you. Watch me." Aponi twisted her body to the left and looked for her left footprint and stepped squarely into it. Then she twisted to the right and found her right print behind her and carefully set her foot in the same place.

"I need something to hold on to," Betty Ann said when she tried it. "I'm going to fall over."

"Put your arms out to balance yourself."

Even so, Betty Ann stumbled and pushed her hands out to break the fall.

As she got up, she said, "Look at those hand prints. That will ruin the whole thing."

"No, it will look like you fell on the way up. They will believe that because it is steep and hard to climb."

It took three times as long to go down, but they made it back to the bushes as the trackers came into sight. The girls ducked down as far as they could.

Horace and Johnny stopped right in front of the bushes.

"Well, they definitely came this way," Johnny said, as he took a long breath. "It looks like they went up here." He started up the hill.

Horace followed, gasping for air. They climbed up to the ledge, but the tracks ended.

"Well, Johnny, where'd they go? What happened?"

Johnny looked up the steep climb in front of them and took a breath. "They think they can out-climb us, so they went up this way on the rocks. That's why the tracks ended, you fool. We'll get them now; those two girls are lost and scared. They can't go much farther."

"Neither can we," Horace moaned, in between puffing and wheezing. "I ain't gonna make it much farther. I can't hardly breathe."

"Come on, old man," Johnny ordered. "You're gonna go as far as it takes. Now move it. Or do you want to do some serious jail time yourself? Kidnapping is a serious offense."

Horace must have been startled by Johnny's attitude, because he took another deep breath and started the climb.

Behind the bushes, Aponi couldn't see Horace and Johnny, but she heard them. Something that Johnny said sparked a memory.

"Is that what ' do time' means? Go to jail?" she whispered to Betty Ann.

"Yeah. Everybody knows that."

Aponi grinned. "Now I understand. Jo did not rob any store or shoot a man. It was that old man, Johnny, your uncle's friend. I heard them talking about it in the truck, and your uncle helped him escape."

Aponi and Betty Ann peeked out of the bushes and watched the men struggle to go up the steep hill, and when they were out of sight, the girls got up and started walking in the opposite direction. Aponi was still worried about not knowing where they were, but she felt somewhat relaxed in the belief that the men were out of the way for good.

While they walked, Aponi told Betty Ann everything she had overheard Horace and Johnny talking about.

CHAPTER 15

THE CLIFF

Jo-Pac finally reached the abandoned lumber mill. He peered through the window of the pickup truck.

"That's Horace Phlegmats' truck. What the heck is he doing way out here, and where are the girls?" he said out loud, while looking it over.

Rifles were hanging from the back window, but not out of place in the country where almost everyone had a rifle rack in their pickup. Blood on the door handle and a bloody blanket in the bed were not common. Four sets of footprints pointed in the direction of the cabin.

"What's going on here?" he said under his breath.

He took one of the rifles from the rack, checked to make sure it was loaded and followed the tracks past the cabin to the rumbling noise coming from the barn. He opened the door slowly. From the crack nearly the entire room could be seen, and no one was in sight. He pushed the door open with force and went inside, rifle first. He stood for a moment at the table holding a half-skinned deer. Then he walked to where the generator hummed and emitted a gasoline stench. He opened one of the freezers.

"This is some serious poaching," he muttered. "The girls stumbled onto a couple of poachers, and one of them is that no-good Horace."

Jo-Pac left the barn and walked around it. At the back there were more footprints leading back to the cabin. He followed them there and kicked the door in. No one was in the front room. He went into the back room. The missing panel could be seen through the hole it left, the hole which had been the escape route for Aponi and Betty Ann.

The girls were still lost but out of harm's way, or so Aponi assumed now that Horace and Johnny were on a wild goose chase up a steep hill. She and Betty Ann trudged on the way to nowhere familiar.

Betty Ann was first to give up. "I can't do this any longer, Aponi. I have to rest for a while. I'm thirsty and I am tired of walking in these dreadful woods. I never go into the woods. And we have no idea where we are going."

Aponi said comfortingly, "I understand; this is a bit much for me also. We will get out of here soon, and then we will take a much needed rest and have some—berries?"

Betty Ann opened her eyes wide. "I want a whole lot more than berries. I want some…"

"I mean berries, over there, it's a berry bush."

The two girls ran over to the bush and attacked it, pulling the fruit off and devouring juicy berries like they hadn't had anything in a week. After eating enough to be satisfied, they threw berries at each other in fun, momentarily forgetting their situation.

A rustling in the bushes put an end to the fun. "Don't make a sound, Betty Ann. It could be your uncle and Johnny."

Aponi moved cautiously toward the sound to investigate. Suddenly the bushes were torn in half, and a big bear's head came growling through. It was a black bear, usually harmless, but dangerous when surprised and hungry. This was one of those times, and somehow Aponi knew it even though she had never seen a live bear.

She jumped back screaming as the angry bear came crashing through the bushes. She ran as fast as she could, dragging a shocked Betty Ann along with her. The bear followed, roaring like nothing Aponi had ever before heard.

Betty Ann found her feet, and the girls ran toward the sound of the river, with the bear getting closer and closer. The path came to an end, and so did the ground. They stopped right at the edge of a cliff that dropped into the river. They turned around and were standing face-to-face with that big, angry black bear. The bear reared up on his hind legs and let out a ferocious roar.

The girls grabbed onto each other and started to cry. *This is the end,* thought Aponi. The bear closed in for the kill, and they shut their eyes and inched farther back. As the bear let out another roar and charged, a shot rang out.

When the girls opened their eyes, the bear was lying dead at their feet. Jo-Pac came running up.

"Are you girls all right?"

Before he got an answer, he was smashed over the head with a stone. He was knocked out, and standing behind him with the stone in his hand was Johnny Blackfoot. Right next to him, holding onto a tree branch and gasping for air, was Horace.

Aponi and Betty Ann screamed and jumped to hug each other. Their combined weight on the jump collapsed the sod overhang, and down they went, right off the cliff.

Johnny grabbed the rifle Jo-Pac had dropped and went over to the edge, aiming to get a shot.

"Can't see 'em," he said. "They must've been pulled under the rapids. They probably hit their heads against that rock sticking out.

He waited for a while, watching the river. After a while he said, "I reckon they're dead."

What he couldn't have known was that the girls never made it into the water. When they fell off the cliff, they hit that rock sticking out, but feet first, and slid onto an inclined ledge about ten feet down.

Aponi had her hand firmly over Betty Ann's mouth, whispering into her ear, "Be quiet. If they hear us, they will kill us both."

Horace went over to the edge of the cliff and looked straight down at the ledge. "Don't see 'em. They must have fallen all the way down."

He turned away from the cliff and looked down at Jo-Pac. "Looks like this old Injun's goin' back to jail for the murder of two little girls."

Johnny answered in a quiet voice, "Yeah, and one crazy old man."

Horace cupped his ear. "Huh? Whacha sayin'?"

"Nothin', Horace. I didn't say a thing. Now let's get this pile of jailbird back to the cabin. We have a lot to do. Grab his legs, and I'll get his arms."

Inside the cabin, Johnny stood guard while Horace went out to the barn for the rope they used to tie up animals. It was bloodstained and crusty with bits of deer flesh. They wrapped it tightly around Jo-Pac's ankles and wrists and threw him into the room where the girls had been. They locked the door, went around back, and Johnny nailed the loose plank back in place.

"That'll hold'im for now," Johnny said as he hammered the last nail in.

"Why do we want to hold him for now? Let's just take him to the law and tell them that we saw him kill them two brats."

"Well," Johnny said, "nobody around here even knows I'm alive, and I am going to keep it that way. Once this all comes out, there's gonna be a big investigation. There'll be police all over this here mountain, and what's gonna happen when they look around here?

You think they gonna let us keep all the skins and meat we got in that barn there? We gotta hide all this stuff, maybe leave a few things to tie Jo-Pac into everything.

"Yeah, that's good."

"Then you call the police and say you were back here looking for the brats and heard them calling out, so you went to see what was going on. That's when you saw him throw them off the cliff, into the river. Ya couldn't save the girls, but you managed to knock him out and lock him up in the cabin. Let's get a move on; we have to load all that stuff into your truck."

Without a word, Horace moved the truck over to the barn.

"Well, look who's giving the orders now and look who's taking them," Johnny said when Horace was too far away to hear him. "Old man, my other plan, the one I didn't tell you about, doesn't have anything to do with your calling the police. You're going to meet the police all right, but as the third body."

Meanwhile, Jimmy made it to Betty Ann's house. The girls weren't there, so he told Betty Ann's mother as much as he knew and asked to borrow the phone to call the police. Jimmy dialed the emergency line while Betty Ann's mother fidgeted and twisted her fingers around a lacy handkerchief.

Jimmy identified himself to the police officer who answered.

"Are you Mike Farrell's boy?" the officer asked. "Your dad knows me. They call me Cork Junior. My dad was a deputy sheriff afore he retired; he knew your granddad."

Jimmy related the story and Jo-Pac's belief that the girls went unwillingly in a truck headed to Old Mill Road.

"Do you mean Jo-Pac the jailbird?" Cork Junior asked. "I don't trust him farther than I can throw a punch. Why shouldn't I think this is a crank call?"

"Because I saw it too and you can take my word for it on my honor and my dad's honor too."

"Okay, kid, calm down. We'll check it out," Cork Junior said. "I'll send a car up to Old Mill Road. Because it's a jailbird, I'll send two cars. I need more details for the report."

Jimmy handed the phone to Betty Ann's mother. "They're going to check out Old Mill Road. They want to know what Betty Ann is wearing. They really need the information from you. I know you're upset, but I've told them all I know, so now I'm going back to help Jo-Pac."

He went through the back yard and the opening in the fence and headed toward Old Mill Road, but hadn't gotten much farther than the stream when he heard the rifle shot that killed the bear. He veered off in that direction and had just about reached the cliff when the sound of an engine startled him. He turned around and saw Horace and Johnny Blackfoot coming his way in a late-model four-wheeler.

Ordinarily Jimmy would have stopped to admire the vehicle, but he had just time enough to get out of sight crouching behind bushes. Johnny was driving, and Horace was sitting in the trailer. The machine stopped with a jerk, and Johnny climbed off and went over to the bear while Horace walked over to the cliff.

"Johnny, you don't think them two brats could have made it, do ya?"

"I don't know. How about if I throw you in, and we see if you make it?"

Then Johnny laughed, an eerie chortle like the way witches laugh. "Let's get to work; I'm not leaving this bearskin behind."

Johnny did the heavy work loading up the bear, and they drove off. When the motor could no longer be heard, Jimmy came out and walked toward the cliff.

Now he put it all together. *They must be poachers, and Jo figured it out. That's why he got so agitated when he saw the truck tracks. But who are the two brats? Could he be talking about Betty Ann, his own niece, and Aponi? And who is that other big Indian? He looks familiar.*

Jimmy ran over to the edge of the cliff and dropped to his knees, worried about what might have happened. He leaned over the edge just as a small hand came up and grabbed a thin branch.

"Hold on to the branch, Betty Ann," a voice from below said. It was Aponi.

Jimmy spoke to them softly so they wouldn't be frightened. "It's Jimmy. I'll help you." Then he moved to the rim and held out his hand. "Take my hand and I'll pull you up."

He lifted Betty Ann up and then Aponi. As soon as they got to their feet, Aponi gave Jimmy a big hug. "I am very happy to see you."

Jimmy was so happy to see her that he hugged her back, but got nervous about it and sheepishly pulled away. "I can't tell you how glad I am to see you both. You had us all worried. I'm just glad that you're safe."

"What would we have done if you hadn't come when you did?"

"You would have fallen back down because that puny little tree root you were climbing up was about to give way." And he tugged on the root to show how it would snap with any more pressure.

Aponi shuddered. "We are lost. Can you please get us out of here?" She started brushing herself off.

Jimmy noticed Betty Ann was standing quietly. "Are you all right, Betty Ann? Are you hurt?" he asked.

Aponi told him Betty Ann was in shock because of all they had gone through, what with being chased to the cliff, and the planning they had heard from Horace and Johnny Blackfoot.

Betty Ann softly said, "They're going to send Jo to jail again, and then they want to kill my whole family."

Aponi filled Jimmy in on the rest of what they had heard. He responded, "I have to save Jo, I have to get there fast."

"What about me and Betty Ann?"

"You're not lost. You're closer than you think. Just go up the river to where the stream joins it and then follow the stream. It's the one that goes back of Betty Ann's house. You'll know the place by the branches you broke on the way there. You're no more than a couple miles away. It's still light; it won't be a problem."

Aponi took Betty Ann's hand, and they started off.

Jimmy walked in the direction that the four-wheeler drove in. He stopped after a few steps and looked back at the two girls. "You understand I have to go after Jo alone."

"I understand," Aponi called over her shoulder.

Betty Ann said nothing.

"Betty Ann's mom needs to know you two are all right," he added as he ran off after the two men and the bear.

CHAPTER 16

THE REUNION

*T*he closer Jimmy got to the cabin, the more scared he became. *After all, I am only thirteen. Well, almost fourteen,* he thought to himself. Then he remembered what his father had said about his military experience, and he found courage.

No one gets left behind, and I'm not going to leave Jo behind.

He went to the corner of the cabin and peeked around the side. He could see Horace and Johnny loading all kinds of animal skins on the truck. *Man, that guy really looks like Jo,* he said to himself as he gave Johnny Blackfoot a good looking-over. *Except, that guy looks like he hasn't had a happy day in his life. I guess that's why him and Horace hang out together.*

A noise came from the cabin; it sounded like scratching. As he moved closer, a plank of wood from the side of the cabin was kicked out right in front of him, almost hitting him in the face. Two booted feet that were tied together came through the hole where the plank had been, then two denim-covered legs. Before the rest of him was outside the cabin, Jimmy recognized Jo-Pac's plaid shirt.

"Jo?" he whispered.

"Help me out here." Jo-Pac's voice on the other side of the wall was muffled but Jimmy knew it was him.

Jimmy found Jo-Pac's knife still in his pocket from when he cut the Red Ring bulb. With two swipes of the sharp pocketknife, he cut through the rope around Jo-Pac's ankles, then helped pull him through and cut the binding at the wrists. They took off and disappeared into the woods.

A little later, Horace came round the cabin mumbling to himself, having been sent by Johnny to investigate a noise. "What right's that there injun got to give me orders? Why, if it weren't fer me, he'd a been rotten away in some cold little cell instead a livin the good life out here."

Horace rambled on, talking to himself as he went into the cabin and checked the door to the other room. It was still closed and locked; but he figured a little taunting would be fun. He opened the door as he slapped an old ax handle against the palm of his hand, like an old-time prison guard.

"How's my Injun inmate doing? What in the...!" The ax handle dropped with a thud.

"Hey, Johnny, he's gone!" Horace shouted from the cabin.

Johnny grabbed both their rifles and ran back behind the cabin. "How'd this happen?"

"It's your fault, you dumb Injun, doncha know how to nail a plank?"

Johnny pulled the hammer back on his rifle. "If I were you, you crazy old man, I would watch what I say. Now let's go get him back. You go that way, and I'll go back this way."

Horace went off on foot, and Johnny hopped on the four-wheeler and took off in another direction.

Jimmy and Jo-Pac were getting farther and farther away. Jimmy related what the girls had said before he sent them back home for help. "So you see, Jo, it was Johnny who shot that guy all those years ago, and you went to jail for it."

"You know, when I was in jail a lot of people confused me with someone called Johnny Blackfoot. He's got to be the same guy, and he is supposed to be very dangerous. I heard a lot of stories about him. Now I can clear my name, and hopefully he will be sent away for good. As for Horace, that no-good—well, I hope he gets what he deserves, too."

Jimmy was tiring out. They had just passed the spot where Jo-Pac was knocked out when Jimmy stepped on some loose muddy ground. He fell and slid down a hill toward the river. Jo-Pac reached for him but missed. Jimmy kept sliding, right off a low cliff and into the river. Jo-Pac ran to the edge of the cliff and looked down at Jimmy rolling down the rapids. He was about to hit some rough water.

"Hold on, Jimmy! I'll be right down!" Jo-Pac turned and walked right into the barrel of a rifle.

"Hello, Injun. Where do ya think you're going?"

Just as he was about hit the white water, Jimmy could see that it was Horace standing on the cliff, gasping for a breath of air and pointing a rifle at Jo-Pac.

"Wave goodbye to him, Injun, he ain't never gonna make it past that waterfalls thatsa commin up. I never liked that kid anyhow, he bothers my dogs. Him and that other brat he's always with, Tommy. Now get walking, we got some unfinished business to take care of. You're goin' to prison again for killing a couple of girls, poaching and hopefully killing that Jimmy, too." He poked Jo-Pac in the back with the rifle barrel.

Below them, Jimmy hit some rough rapids and tried to grab anything he could to pull himself up and keep his head above the water.

He reached for a branch hanging over the river, but the force was too strong, and he couldn't cling to it. The river was raging, and the water twisted and bounced him off rocks while it carried him away.

Surely, there is no coming back from this one, he thought as his whole adventure was flashing before his eyes. He thought of Tommy, who might never be big again, the Takoda Indian tribe, Aponi and the friendship that would never happen. He hoped his mother wouldn't cry; he knew his father would be strong.

Then a log bumped him, and he held onto it. He closed his eyes. It felt like the water was slowing down. *This must be the end. It feels so peaceful like I am just drifting; the falls must be coming up.* After a while he couldn't feel the water move at all. He opened his eyes. He was floating in a calm pool.

A musty smell was in the air, and a low roar sounded like distant thunder—*the rapids*. He could see grass and trees, and suddenly he realized he was soaked and bruised—and alive. *This must be the only calm water anywhere near here. I'm glad I made my way over here instead of the falls.*

He pulled himself out of the water and lay down on the shore. He was so worn out that he wasn't sure that he could even get up. Then he heard Aponi's voice in his head. "The body feels the way the mind tells it to feel."

He pulled himself to his feet and staggered up the hill. As he climbed, he repeated again and again, "I know I can make it. I know I will save Jo. There is no way that evil Horace Phlegmats is going to beat us, not this time." Jimmy felt stronger with each step he took.

Finding the place where he fell in was the only way he was going to get back to the cabin. But he was just as lost as the two girls were so deep in those woods. All he knew was he had to go upriver to find Jo-Pac.

At the same time, Horace was forcing Jo-Pac to walk to the cabin. Horace poked him in the back with the rifle every couple of steps.

"So, Injun, ya think you'll ever see the outside of a prison again? I don't think so. I reckon this time they're gonna throw away the key, and I for one won't miss ya at all, maybe you'll even get a death sentence."

Jo-Pac didn't say anything. Horace talked enough for both of them. "Ya know, Injun, you really do look an awful lot like ol' Johnny Blackfoot, the two of ya could be brothers. If I didn't know any better, I'd say that you were bro…"

At this, Horace lost his footing on some leaves covering a shallow depression in the ground. Jo-Pac wasted no time in leaving him behind. Horace stood up quickly, got his balance and took a couple of shots. He missed every time, and Jo-Pac made it into the thick bushes.

As he ran into a clearing, he nearly ran into Johnny sitting on the four-wheeler, with the rifle pointed right at him.

"So, if it ain't the one-and-only, Mr. Jo-Pac. Pleased to make your acquaintance. I have heard so much about you—not to mention the thanks I owe you for the twenty years. I know, I know, no thanks necessary. And now you'll be going back for murdering three people and poaching. Shame on you."

"Why are you such an evil man, Johnny? Indians are taught better than this. You know right from wrong, yet you choose wrong. You choose to slither like a snake instead of soaring like an eagle."

"Shut up! You sound just like our father," Johnny shouted angrily.

Jo-Pac's jaw dropped and he stared at Johnny.

"That's right, Jolon," Johnny continued, "and I see you took our father's name, too. Paco. It's me, Patamon, your older brother, the one our father didn't want. Well, I didn't want him, either, or the rest of that Takoda tribe of orphan Indians. I left when I had the chance. I knew father was going to make you Chief. He told me he knew on the day I was born that I was no good. He told me my eyes were as those of a mad dog, full of anger. That is why he called me Patamon, and sometimes he said it in English because it sounded so much worse in the tongue of the visitors. 'Raging,' he called me, like the river. He said

I could never lead the tribe; as a chief I would bring our people much pain and suffering. So I left it all behind. I ate one of those bulbs, took a new name, and lived my own life, far away from all of you and your peace loving way of life."

"I thought you were dead, Patamon. That is what father said when he came back to the village alone after the hunting trip."

"Yes, well, he told me that I was dead also, dead to him. That was when he caught me aiming an arrow at you before we left to hunt. I would have shot you then, but he took my bow. That whole tribe, you and our father included, are too naive to realize you cannot have peace in life. If you want something, you must take it and make it yours. When I heard about your getting arrested, I figured it was you, my brother, coming to look for me. The flowers are growing again, aren't they? You know for a while, I looked for them. I was going to go back and kill you, but when I heard that you went to jail, I was much happier seeing the future Chief in jail. I knew it would kill you to be locked away from your people."

Jo-Pac challenged, "They are our people."

"No," Johnny said, "they are your people. I have no people. Why didn't you go back when you got out?"

Jo-Pac bowed his head. "I wanted to, but it was so long. I figured that when I told my son Yuma to watch our people, he was doing a good job. And that if I went back and was made Chief, he would want to see this world for himself. I didn't ever want any of our people to go through what I went through, especially my own son."

Johnny sat back down on the vehicle and started it up. "All right, Jolon, enough of this family reunion, time to go back and face your destiny. I'll tell you what, after this is all over, I just might go back as you. There isn't anyone who will question me, I'm the Chief. No one there, or here, will know the difference."

Jo-Pac looked at him and scowled. "What about your old pal Horace? Oh, I get it, Horace is the third person I'm going to go to jail for killing. Why would you do all this, just because you weren't going to be Chief? Aren't you bothered to take the life of another man?"

Johnny turned off the motor and climbed down. "Let me tell you what bothers me, brother. It's being a young brave driven out from his home, coming into this giant world totally without a clue. I was treated like dirt, less then dirt. I spent a lot of years traveling, and every place I went, I was treated the same. So, just as I lived in the village, I lived in this world. I took what I wanted and did whatever I had to do to get it. By the time I came back to this town, my first town in this world, I hated all of these people, the white men just as I hated the Takoda Indians. The only reason I let Horace stay alive this long is because I needed him. But now I am going home. I know where I have to go, after I find one of those flowers and eat it. You see, another reason Horace was such a help was that he sees little Indians on his land. Everyone thinks that he's crazy. I don't. I think he showed me the way home. Until now, I figured that I was the only one who believed him. Enough talking, let's go."

Jo-Pac sputtered a protest, but Johnny became more forceful. "I said, let's go." He left the vehicle where it was and walked back, following Jo-Pac with the rifle pointed at his back.

CHAPTER 17

TOMMY WAKES UP

$\mathcal{S}$ome time earlier that day in the Takoda village, the medicine man moved Tommy into the hut where Jimmy had stayed. Tommy had regained consciousness, despite the medicine man's belief that he would not wake from the sleeping sickness.

Yuma came in and stood next to the cot. Tommy was groggy but hungry. Yuma's sons brought food, and Tommy was able to sit up and answer some of the Chief's questions.

Yuma had come to believe that Jimmy kidnapped his daughter to trade for Tommy. He didn't want to believe it because he liked Jimmy, but all he could think about was what his father had said all those years ago: "If I do not return, the giant world is a bad place and no one else must go there."

Yuma knew that Aponi was curious about the giant world but never thought she would disobey him. He wanted to look for his daughter, but decided to wait until he could learn from Tommy what to expect in the giant world.

"You are all right, still sick?" Yuma asked as Tommy devoured the meal.

Tommy rubbed his head and looked up at Yuma. "I'm okay, but where am I? And where is Jimmy? And who are you?"

"I am Yuma, son of Jolon, and this is my village. Plain Old Jimmy left with Aponi, daughter of Yuma. Jimmy left you when you are sick, why? You must tell me where he went, and why did he take Aponi?"

"I don't know. Since I was sick, he probably went to get Jo. He's the one Jimmy always calls when we're in trouble."

Yuma bent over Tommy. "Who is this Jo? Why do they go see him?"

Tommy shrugged his shoulders. "I don't know why. Jo's a crazy old indi—I mean Jo is an old Abenaki Indian who helps Jimmy out of trouble sometimes."

Yuma moved closer to Tommy. "He is Abenaki? Where does he live?"

Tommy fell back to sleep. Yuma told the medicine man to take good care of Tommy, and to feed him again when he woke up, but not to allow him to leave the hut.

While Tommy slept, the braves Yuma had sent to find Aponi returned. Yuma was in the stable brushing Nodin, Aponi's horse that made his way back to the village. When they walked in, Akando and Dyami told him all they knew from their trip.

"We follow trail for a long way," began Akando, "past the place where we get so-ga. The prints stop by water; we think they cross to other side. Maybe Plain Old Jimmy have some rope."

Dyami continued the story. "So we went across water to look, but we do not find trail. We keep looking and find this."

In Dyami's hand was a big piece of a bulb from the Red Ring

flower. "I have never seen Magic Red Ring flower, but one day your father tell me how it looks. We dig hole and cut this from root; this have magic in it."

Akando spoke again. "If Chief Yuma want, Akando and Dyami will eat magic and go find daughter."

Yuma knew neither brave was anxious to go, but they each would do anything for their Chief and the safety of his daughter, including risking their own lives by going into the giant world. Yuma took the piece of bulb from Dyami and sent them away and squatted down in thought for a while. After a few moments he stood up and called the braves back.

"Aponi is my daughter; I will go. Other boy, Tommy, he will go too. Tell medicine man make some sleep juice."

What was most important to Yuma, even more important than his own daughter Aponi, was the survival of his people. As Chief, that is what he had to think of before anything else.

Yuma knew he could not let Tommy know the location of their village or that they were shrunken. He didn't seem to remember anything about his size, and Yuma wanted to keep it that way. If they were going into the giant world, Tommy must be sleeping when they left the village.

Back by the river, Jimmy was getting closer to where he fell in. The landscape started to look familiar, so he cut into the woods. As he made his way back to the path, he heard footsteps coming his way. He hid under a fallen tree. There was total silence, and he thought the danger had passed. As he stepped out, a hand came around the tree and covered his mouth.

"Plain Old Jimmy, where is Aponi?" Yuma asked as he took his hand away from Jimmy's mouth.

"Yuma, am I glad to see you. Wait, how did you get here, how did you know where to find me?" Then he saw Tommy in the torn chambray shirt, coming out from behind another tree.

"Tommy!" Jimmy yelled. "You're all right! Last time I saw you, you were out like a light."

Yuma whispered into Jimmy's ear, "He does not know about village or Magic Red Ring. You will not tell him."

Jimmy nodded, but was confused. *How couldn't he know? He had to leave the village and eat another bulb. How could he have not noticed anything different?*

"Hey, Jimmy, where did you go? Why did you leave me in that cool village? It's great how they all moved into a big cave, isn't it? I'd like to go back one day. Was it very far? Yuma said that I slept the whole way back. All I remember was that after we ate, I went to sleep and woke up near the tractor bridge, riding on a horse with Yuma. By the way, a horse called Nodin is tied up by our campsite behind your house."

Before Jimmy could say anything, Yuma asked again, "Where is Aponi? Why did you take her from village?"

"It was the only way she would tell me where to go. She said that she was at the fishing hole before, and if I took her, she would show me the way. You understand, don't you? I had to help my friend. You don't have to worry about Aponi. She was lost, but I found her and sent her back to Betty Ann's house. She's safe, and she's probably there now. By the way, how did you guys know where to find me?"

Tommy piped up, "I took him over to your house. Don't worry, your mom didn't see him. She said she got a call from Betty Ann's mom, and you were with Jo, looking for them in the woods or something."

"We have to go help Jo, he's in trouble." Jimmy started to tell them what happened, but Yuma cut him off.

"We will go get Aponi now. I must take her home."

"Please, Yuma, I'm telling you that Jo is in trouble, you have to help. The only reason he got into this trouble is because he came with me to help find Aponi. If we don't help him, he's going to die."

Yuma was silent for a minute or two, then he said he would go to help Jo.

"Okay Plain Old Jimmy, we will go help friend. If I do not help someone in trouble, especially another Indian, I do not bring honor to my father. I am Chief Yuma, son of Jolon, I will do as my father before me would do."

CHAPTER 18

THE RESCUE

Johnny and Jo-Pac were just about at the cabin when Johnny called out, "Horace, where are you, old man?" There was no answer, so he led Jo-Pac into the barn past the humming generator and handcuffed him around a support column.

"Don't worry, Jolon, it won't be long before you're back in that nice comfortable cell. All we have to do is wait for your next victim."

Just as he said that, Horace stuck his head in the barn door. "Guess what, Johnny, I have a surprise for you."

Horace came in all the way, holding onto a rope. As he pulled on it, in stumbled Aponi and Betty Ann. Their hands were tied up at the end of the rope.

Jo-Pac reacted immediately. "You know what you want, Patamon.

I'll tell you where you can find the flower. You can just go back to the village and take my place. You don't have to kill anybody."

Johnny laughed that evil-witch laugh. "I know that I don't have to, but I really want to. Don't worry, Jolon, I'll let you watch."

Aponi's eyes opened wide at the name Jolon. She started to say something, but Jo-Pac signaled her to be quiet. Horace dragged the girls over to the column where Jo-Pac was bound.

As he passed Johnny, Horace handed his rifle over, "Hold on to this, I'm gonna tie the girls to the pole."

"Where'd you find 'em?" Johnny asked.

"I asked ya, ya dumb Injun, you think they could of made it. No, ya said, they're dead. Well, I guess you were wrong again. If you ain't the dumbest Injun."

Horace blabbered on as he kneeled and tied them to the pole. When he was done, he stood and turned around. There Johnny was, pointing Horace's rifle at his chest.

Terror covered Horace's face. "Now hold on, Inj—I mean Johnny. I didn't mean nothin' by that. Our plan is right on target."

Johnny smiled at him. "You're right. The plan is coming along fine."

Jo-Pac said, "That's right, Horace, the plan is for you to be my final victim, and Johnny gets away with everything."

Horace laughed in a half-convinced way. Then sweat started pouring down his face. "He's kidding, right? Johnny, answer me."

Johnny just laughed.

"What did I ever do to you, Johnny? I was your only friend. I helped you out more times than I can remember, we're pals."

Johnny stopped laughing and poked him in the chest with his rifle. "I have no friends, no pals, nothing. You may have helped me in the past, but where I'm going, I won't need your help. I don't need you anymore."

Johnny pulled the hammer back, and just as he was about to pull the trigger, a police siren sounded followed by a voice on a bullhorn, echoing on the hills.

Johnny turned in the direction of the siren, and Horace pushed the rifle away. It went off. He jumped on Johnny, knocking him to the ground. As the two men wrestled, Jo-Pac worked at the girls' ropes with his cuffed hands as a voice came over the bullhorn.

"This is the state police. We have the place surrounded. Come out with your hands up."

Then Johnny hit Horace over the head with the rifle stock. Horace lay lifeless. Johnny stood up and aimed at Jo-Pac.

"At least I can take you with me, little brother." He pulled the hammer back again and laughed. "Do you have any last words?"

An arrow shot from a bow whizzed in through the open door and into Johnny's arm, knocking the rifle away. The rifle went off a second time. Johnny fell to his knees screaming as the police came in the door. Two officers grabbed Johnny, then handcuffed him and Horace and led them out of the barn. Two other troopers went over and untied Aponi and Betty Ann.

Aponi knelt and rubbed her wrists where the ropes had been. Betty Ann stooped over her. "Are you okay?"

"Just a little rope burn. It will be all right."

Jo-Pac was still attached to the pole. "You got any handcuff keys out there?" one of the rescuers called out after trying his own key.

"Not that kind," another officer answered.

"Look in Johnny's shirt pocket, that's where he put them," Jo-Pac said.

A set of keys on a ring was tossed in the door and landed on the table where the deer was still half-butchered. "Try one of these," an unseen officer said.

Betty Ann ran over to get it. "Eew," she groaned while scrunching up her nose, but she bravely put her hand out and recovered the keys from beside the deer's head and delivered them to the officer.

While Jo-Pac was being freed, Jimmy, Tommy and Yuma strode into the barn like the heroes they were.

Betty Ann ran over to Tommy and wrapped her arms around him. "Am I glad to see you, but what are you doing here?"

Tommy blushed and took her by the hand and led her out of the barn. "I'll tell you all about it after we tell your mother that you're all right."

"Yes, let's get out of this dreadful place," Betty Ann sighed.

Aponi ran over to Jimmy and gave him a big hug and a kiss on the cheek. "I knew you would save me. Every time I was scared, I thought of you. I thought about you and what you said to me when we saw the moon last night, how you would always think of me when you looked at the moon. That gave me courage."

Yuma and Jo-Pac watched the reunions without noticing each other until Aponi ran to her father and gave him a hug.

"I am sorry, father, but I had to do what I thought was right. I wanted to go with him to see this beautiful world."

Yuma got down on one knee and hugged Aponi tightly, pulled her away, and looked into her face. "This is not a beautiful world, this is a dangerous world. There is nothing here for us."

Aponi pulled away. "There is Jimmy, my friend." Then she walked over to Jo-Pac and looked up at him. "And there is my grandfather, Jolon."

A single tear rolled down Jo-Pac's cheek. He picked her up in his arms. "And here is my granddaughter."

Yuma said, "Why do you call her granddaughter?"

Jo-Pac put Aponi down and walked over to Yuma. A look of familiarity came over his face. "Father? You are Jolon? You are Jolon."

"I am sorry, my son. I hope you can forgive me." He offered his hand for Yuma to shake.

Yuma took a step back as if in thought for few seconds, then he pushed Jo's hand away and hugged him. "You are my father, you do not need to ask me to forgive. You only need to ask for your son's love, he will always love you."

Jimmy stepped into the middle of the reunion. "Can somebody please tell me what is going on? I am so lost, I don't think I'm hearing correctly."

Aponi led him away. "I will tell you all about it." She lifted his hand, the one she was holding, and looked at him with a stunned expression. "Hey, you do not turn red when I hold your hand anymore." They both laughed and walked outside still holding hands.

Yuma and Jo-Pac were right behind them, the father beginning to tell his son about the past thirty or so years. When they got outside, Jo-Pac told the police everything that happened, except where Johnny was from.

It was getting dark by the time Betty Ann's mother drove up. "The police called me, I'm so glad you're all right." She cried and fussed like she hadn't seen Betty Ann in years, not just a few hours. She held the seat for Tommy to get in the back, and then lifted Betty Ann like a child and put her into the front seat. "I'll drop Tommy off on my way. Seatbelts, everyone," she said as they went off.

Aponi, Yuma, and Jimmy waited for Jo-Pac to finish speaking with the police. There was total silence among the three of them, all deep in thought. Jimmy was thinking about how much more time he and Aponi would have together, and something told him she was thinking about pretty much the same thing. Yuma's eyes were wide like he was still in shock over everything that happened today and all the different things that he was seeing in this giant world.

Jo-Pac finished and joined them. "Well, this is a good day after all. I've met my granddaughter, been reunited with my son, and my name is cleared. Johnny got Horace so scared that he is over there spilling his guts about everything. He even told the police that the car in the barn was the one he stole when he picked up Johnny after the shooting all those years ago. They are going to jail for a very long time."

Yuma stood up, as if to start walking, but Jo-Pac stopped him with a raised arm.

"The state troopers are going to take us home. After we get to my house, I'll walk you home, Jimmy. I can't drive you because my truck is still at Betty Ann's house. I spoke with your mother on the police phone. She hadn't heard anything since Betty Ann's mom called her this afternoon, but she's fine now. Yuma, you and Aponi will stay the night with me. We will talk and get to know each other. I know that you must be worried about the village, but it would be very dangerous for you if you go back in darkness."

Yuma smiled and nodded. "I would like to know my father more, but why do we wait, why do we not go to your home now?"

Jo-Pac said, "The police are going to give us a ride. It is far from here, and the children are tired after such a long day."

"How will we ride? I see no horses, no wagons."

Jimmy, Jo-Pac and Aponi all laughed.

Aponi explained, "It is horseless wagon, father. It moves even faster than Nodin, but it does make a lot of noise."

A car rolled up next to them. Yuma jumped back from the iron monster. He went for his bow and arrow, ready to defend all.

"No, Yuma, this machine is going to take us home." Jo-Pac guided him into the car, opening the back door. Yuma seemed reluctant to get in.

"At least this is quieter than the other one," Aponi said.

They got in and closed the doors. The car took off, with Aponi and Yuma sitting in the back seat on either side of Jimmy. Both looked uncomfortable. When the car stopped, the trooper and Jo-Pac got out and opened the doors to the back. Yuma jumped out quickly and turned around to look at the iron horse. Aponi climbed out from the other side, followed by Jimmy.

"What a wonderful hut grandfather lives in," she said when she saw the house.

Jo-Pac gave them a quick tour, and they marveled at the luxury in which he lived.

"Look, father, there is even a spring for washing," Aponi said, turning on the faucet at the kitchen sink.

Jo-Pac told them to get comfortable in the living room and he would be right back. "Come on, Jimmy, I've got to get you home."

Jimmy looked at Jo-Pac and then at Aponi. Before he could say a word, Aponi asked why Jimmy had to leave.

"He can come back tomorrow to say goodbye, but for now he has to go home to his mother. She is worried."

Aponi turned around with her head down, and Jimmy walked out the door the same way. Jo-Pac and Yuma smiled at each other and gave each other an understanding nod.

"I would ask you to stay for supper," Jo-Pac said, "but your mother wants you home."

Supper. What a wonderful word. Jimmy suddenly felt hungry as a bear as he realized he had nothing to eat since the blueberries and sour-cream-and-onion chips of that morning.

"Yeah, my mother will have supper waiting," Jimmy said as he hurried home.

CHAPTER 19

BACK TO THE VILLAGE

𝒯he next day, Jimmy was at Jo-Pac's house bright and early. He stepped up to the door with a great big smile on his face and knocked. There was no answer, so he knocked again just as Jo-Pac opened the door.

"Hey, Jimmy. Sorry, I was on the phone with Mr. Phlegmats."

"Hi," Jimmy said as he walked past Jo-Pac. "Where is she? What happened to Aponi?"

The phone rang. "Hold on, Jimmy. Let me get that."

Jo-Pac answered the phone and talked for a couple of minutes that seemed like a couple of years to Jimmy. As he hung up the phone, Jimmy ran over to him and grabbed his arm.

"Tell me, Jo, where is Aponi?"

"Well, Jimmy, she went back to the village with Yuma. He had to get his horse and get back to his people."

"What!" The world crashed down on him. He didn't even get a chance to say goodbye.

"Oh yeah, Jimmy, that was your mother on the phone. It seems that your father is coming back from his trip early. There's a problem with your aunt out west, so he's going to pack up the car for an early family vacation."

Jimmy shook his head. "There is no way I want to spend my summer with Aunt Donna. She makes me crazy."

Jo started to laugh. "I think your mother knows how you feel. That's why she agreed with me that you would have a better experience spending the summer visiting my family."

Jimmy smiled a smile that felt like it covered his whole face. "You mean we're going back to the village with Aponi? We're going to stay there for the whole summer?"

"Well, not the whole summer. I have to get back for the last week of August. The Phlegmats want me to take over that farm of theirs since Horace is on permanent leave."

"That's great. You deserve it after all you went through because of that old creep and his friend."

Jimmy realized he was talking about Jo-Pac's brother. "Sorry, I didn't mean anything..."

"That's okay. That man wasn't my brother. My brother died a long time ago; his soul did anyway. That man just looked like him. Enough about that. Don't you have to pack? And remember, not a word about the Takoda tribe. You're the only one that knows of them besides me, since Tommy doesn't remember a thing about the Magic Red Ring."

Jimmy ran over to the door and opened it. "You got it, Jo. I'll see you in a few."

He ran all the way home, thinking about the wonderful summer he was going to have. He packed quickly, said goodbye to his mother, and called his father to say goodbye. After that, he was out the door and headed to Jo-Pac's house.

This time, they pulled out two Magic Red Ring flowers and brought them to the slate mountain before eating one. The other they tucked into a crevice to have when they left. They fell asleep next to the stream and woke up next to the river, with Yuma, Akando, Anoki and Dyami there to greet them.

"Hello, Plain Old Jimmy," Yuma said. "Welcome. I must thank you. Aponi has told me you were a good friend to her, and you kept her safe."

The other Indian braves welcomed him one at a time by shaking his hand, then went and bowed to Jo-Pac, whom they called Jolon. He bowed back, and then he put out his hand in friendship. They all shook hands and chattered to each other as they headed inside the mountain. Once they passed through the tunnel, Aponi was waiting to greet them. She ran over and gave her grandfather a hug and a kiss; then she went over to Jimmy and grinned.

"Come on, Jimmy, I will show you to your shelter."

As they walked down the trail hand in hand, her father and grandfather watched and smiled.

It made him feel grown-up to have a hut all his own. Of course, the hut was for sleeping, and everyone in the village gathered in the common areas for day-to-day activities.

Aponi and Jimmy spent a lot of time together. He taught her some arithmetic, world history, and about the giant world. She was already okay with her reading and writing.

He also spent a lot of time with the other young braves in the village. By the end of the summer, he had become quite a young brave himself. He learned Indian ways, became an expert tracker, and was the best canoe-tipper in the whole village.

Jimmy and Aponi knew they would soon have to say goodbye at summer's end. On the last day, they sat by the pond just staring into the water. Both of them wore long faces.

"Jimmy, I will miss you very much; you are my best friend. I will be very sad tomorrow watching you leave."

Jimmy turned to her and held both her hands. "I know; this was the best summer I ever had in my life. I learned so much here, I feel like an Indian brave. I feel like I belong here, I belong with you."

They walked back to Jimmy's shelter in silence. When they got there, Aponi looked at him with tears building in her eyes. She kissed him on the cheek and ran away. Jimmy did all that he could not to cry himself. He went into the shelter with his head down, trying to be strong.

The next morning as Jo-Pac and Jimmy were getting ready to go, Aponi could not be found. She was hiding in the saddlebag school, with all her books, crying.

As they left the village, Jimmy shook his head in disappointment. "I can't believe she didn't come to say goodbye."

Jo-Pac said, "You know, you can come back next summer and spend some time at the village again."

After they ate a piece of the bulb from the Red Ring flower again, they fell asleep outside the slate mountain, with the Indian braves watching over them for protection. They woke up, back at their normal size, and walked home. Jimmy was still quiet, thinking all the way back, *This is the second time she didn't say goodbye.* He did, at least, say goodbye to Jo-Pac when they reached the Farrell house. The car in the driveway told Jimmy his parents were back from their trip. All this time, and he never once thought about Aunt Donna's trouble.

"Okay, Jimmy, enjoy your last two weeks of summer, and tell your parents I said hello."

"Will do, Jo, see ya later," he said as he went onto the front porch with his head down, still wearing a long face. Before he went in he turned to Jo-Pac. "Hey, I just figured it out, the bulb makes you fall asleep while your body changes, right?"

"That's right, Jimmy," Jo-Pac said as he waved goodbye.

CHAPTER 20

SUMMER'S END

"Tommy is on the phone," Jimmy's mother said.

"I don't want to talk to him right now," Jimmy answered.

"At least say hello. Friendships have to be nurtured." She put the phone in Jimmy's hand.

Yeah, I know, he thought, *and that's why she didn't say goodbye twice.* "Hey, Tommy. What's up?"

"Where have you been all summer? Did you go out west to see your Aunt Donna?"

"I didn't go. I spent the summer with Jo and Yuma and Aponi."

"Yeah? How come I didn't see you?"

"We were at the Takoda village."

"Where *is* that cave? I was looking on a map and didn't see a reservation."

"I'm not allowed to say."

"Maybe Jo will tell me. He works for Betty Ann's parents now."

"I know. That's why we had to come back early. I would have called you but I've been sick, sorry."

"That's okay Jimmy. So, wanna go fishing?"

"Nah, I just don't feel like it."

"There's something seriously wrong with you."

"Yeah, I guess," Jimmy said.

"I've been pretty busy myself, with Betty Ann. I've been hanging out with her the whole summer. She's like my girlfriend now, isn't that great?"

"Yea, Tommy, I'm happy for you. Well, I gotta go."

"Okay, Jimmy, I'll see ya!"

Tommy spent the last two weeks of summer hanging out with Betty Ann. Jimmy did nothing but stay in his room and think about Aponi and the rest of the Takoda tribe. He missed them terribly, but he knew he had to get on with his life and prepare to live without them. He called Tommy the last day of summer vacation just to catch up with him and tell him he would see him on the bus in the morning.

The next morning they met on the bus and talked mostly about Tommy getting close to Betty Ann after the rescue. Jimmy said little; he was just listening to Tommy and thinking about Aponi.

When they got to school, Jimmy got off the bus and stared at the big brick building. "Here goes another year, my first year in high school."

Then he recognized Jo-Pac by the office and went over to say hello. "Hey Jo, what are you doing here?"

"I had some business in town. Since I was here anyway, I figured I would say hello."

"What brings you to town?"

"Remember Horace's dogs, Satan and Lucifer? Well, with Horace gone, they wouldn't eat and made themselves sick. So I took them to the vet to be put down."

"That's no loss. Those were some evil dogs." Jimmy declared.

"You know Jimmy, Aponi is also glad they're gone."

"Have you seen her? How is she?"

"Why don't you ask her yourself?"

A familiar, soft voice called Jimmy's name. He turned around and was pleasantly surprised.

"Aponi! What are you doing here?"

"Surprise! I go to school here now."

"How can you?"

"My grandfather talked my father into letting me go to school," she said excitedly. "They agreed it would be good for me, and I could bring knowledge of today's world back to the tribe."

"She took all the tests," Jo-Pac said with grandfatherly pride, "and the school said she will be placed in your grade. Thanks to all the teaching you did over the summer."

Jimmy couldn't believe it. It was like Christmas and his birthday rolled into one. He took one of Aponi's hands, as he was used to doing by now, and led her into the school building.

"Let's go find Tommy and Betty Ann. They will be so surprised."

"Guess what, Jimmy? My grandfather says Betty Ann's grandparents went south to Florida, where bananas come from."

Jimmy laughed. "That's right."

He squeezed her hand. "This is going to be the best year ever. We're going to have a great time."

"Until the next adventure?" she said.

"I'm through with adventures," Jimmy said with an air of assurance. "No more adventures for me. Not ever again. No-o way."